D0471209

A Hungarian Romance

a novel by

Ágnes Hankiss

Translated with an Introduction
by Emma Roper-Evans

Foreword by
Professor Marianna Birnbaum

readers international

The title of this book in Hungarian is *Széphistória*, first published in 1988 by Artunion/Széchenyi Könyvkiadó publishers of Budapest.
© Ágnes Hankiss 1988

First published in English by Readers International Inc, Columbia, Louisiana and Readers International, London. Editorial inquiries to the London office at 8 Strathray Gardens, London NW3 4NY England. US/Canadian inquiries to the Subscriber Service Department, P.O.Box 959, Columbia LA 71418-0959 USA.
English translation © Readers International Inc 1992

This translation was made possible in part through grant support from the Central and East European Publishing Project and the Arts Council of Great Britain. The editors also wish to thank Eva Palotai and Anne O'Brien for their assistance in preparing this book.

Cover illustration: *Flora* (ca. 1591) by the 16th century Hapsburg court painter Giuseppe Arcimboldo
Cover design by Jan Brychta
Printed and bound in the UK by Clays Ltd, Bungay

Library of Congress Catalog Card Number: 91-60881

British Library Cataloguing in Publication Data
Ágnes Hankiss
A Hungarian Romance: a novel
1. Hungarian fiction
I. Title II. Szephistoria. *English*
894. 51133

ISBN 0-930523-81-4 Hardcover
ISBN 0-930523-82-2 Paperback

Foreword

On the surface A Hungarian Romance *, Ágnes Hankiss'*
first novel, is about a passionate love triangle of two men
and a woman, their joy, anguish and treachery, played
out against the backdrop of a violent seventeenth-century
Transylvania.

However, this masterfully layered book has more
ambitious goals. Hankiss is preoccupied with the invisible
history of the "universal soul" and with the problem of
the eternally returning archetype as it can be represented
in literature. That is why she turned from her chosen
profession, psychology - of the Jungian kind - to belles
lettres, *where the cognitive sciences impose no limitations*
on her creative talent.

Hankiss is fascinated by the process, as she puts it
elsewhere, "how each link fits into the eternal chain of
history", by which she does not mean a spatial or
temporal completeness. In her concept a random word or
an abortive gesture may have more profound meaning or
value as truth than entire biographies or precisely
described sequences of action. Nothing is inconsequen-
tial, no matter how tiny; nothing that has ever existed can
be anachronistic. In her novel Hankiss moves freely
among people, places and periods because for her
everything is connected. Just as public history invades the
private sphere, so does the eternal break into the

temporal and into its soul space.

Hankiss' work is even more remarkable for being written in a country where until recently originality was suspect, and where women's role in life and letters has for centuries been relegated to backstage. A Hungarian Romance *is bold and liberated in spirit, and entirely independent artistically. Hankiss draws on the best narrative traditions of Hungarian fiction, but she does so in order to subvert them for her own stylistic purposes. In the novel, baroque prose alternates with spare discourse, underscoring or restraining the tension created by the protagonists and by history.*

Regarding the author's role in the text, Hankiss believes in "a state of grace" and in the unavoidable mirroring of a part of herself in each of her characters. Thus to the question of what is autobiographical in this novel, she can honestly answer, "Everything and nothing".

Above all Hankiss makes it clear for the reader that an artist has been here, and that the artist is more important than any subject. This is, I submit, the essence of modernity in the arts.

Prof. Marianna Birnbaum
Slavic Department
University of California
Los Angeles

Introduction

Ágnes Hankiss' novel consists of two discrete narratives, a "history" and a "herstory". The former is a fictionalised account of real events, wherein all the characters mentioned actually existed. The latter is a domestic drama, therefore invisible in the history books. Hankiss' powerful "herstory" speaks for itself; but it is necessary to give some background to the "History Lessons" in this book, for the benefit of those readers not familiar with Hungary's complex past.

During the historical period covered by the novel, Hungary was divided into three parts. The Battle of Mohács in 1526 - where King Louis of Hungary was defeated by Suleiman the Magnificent - resulted in nearly two centuries of partition for Hungary. The Turks occupied the heartland of the country, leaving the western fringes of the kingdom to be fought over by local magnates and Ferdinand of Hapsburg, who claimed the Hungarian throne after Louis had perished on the battlefield. Following two decades of fighting, in which the Turkish government of Hungary (the Porte) was also involved, Ferdinand concluded a truce with the Sultan which recognised the Hapsburg claim to the northern and western edges of Hungary in return for tribute paid annually to Constantinople.

Moreover, in 1566 the Sultan proclaimed Transylvania

to be an autonomous principality under his own suzerainty. This allowed the Transylvanians to elect their own ruler, subject to Turkish approval. The spirit of Hungarian national independence was thus kept alive in Transylvania, albeit precariously; for the region was subject to both Hapsburg manipulation and local struggles for power.

When *A Hungarian Romance* opens, in the last decade of the sixteenth century, the Turks occupy most of the old kingdom, the Hapsburg Emperor Rudolf controls its western periphery (to which most of the Hungarian nobility have fled), and Transylvania is ruled by Krisztof Báthory, who is hostile to the Hapsburgs because of their repeated interference in his territory.

The novel begins with a conversation about Mátyás Corvinus, ruler of Hungary from 1458-1490. He was a true Renaissance prince who married the daughter of the King of Naples and represented the old glory and culture of Hungary. The Forgách cousins compare the Mátyás of old with the present Hapsburg Archduke Mátyás and his brother, the eccentric and much distrusted Emperor Rudolf.

For his part Rudolf certainly had little regard for the glories of the Magyar past. He transferred his court from Vienna (where Hungarian affairs were dealt with by the chancellery set up by Ferdinand) to Prague, where Hungarian business could reach the court only at second hand. Moreover, the Emperor was at loggerheads with the Hungarians on religious grounds. After Mohács the spirit of the Reformation, and Protestantism in particular, made inroads into Hungarian society at all levels, especially as many important Catholics had died during the prolonged hostilities. Protestantism even came to embody a spirit of independence in the face of Hapsburg might. By contrast Rudolf's own cousins and uncles had initiated the Counter-Reformation in Inner Austria and the Tyrol, and this surely would have increased his natural antipathy toward the new doctrine.

Ágnes Hankiss draws a vivid historical picture of Emperor Rudolf at his court in Prague, surrounded by astrologists and scientists (Kepler was one of his circle), searching for the Philosopher's Stone and probing the mysteries of the Cabbala. He was also an avid art collector, and readers of *Utz* will remember that the author Bruce Chatwin's initial desire to visit Prague was inspired by Rudolf's passion for exotica.

Rudolf's clique of military advisors viewed the Hungarians as a band of insolent rebels who should be neutralised at all costs, an attitude which was aggravated by the outbreak in 1591 of the Fifteen Years War. Essentially a conflict with the Turks, it was complicated by the emergence of Transylvania as a distinct political power. By this time Transylvania was controlled by Zsigmond Báthory (Krisztof's son), another unstable character like Rudolf who had allied himself with the Hapsburgs in return for the hand of Rudolf's cousin, Maria Christina.

The Emperor could thus avail himself of the resources of both Transylvania and Hapsburg Hungary, and he felt he could act with impunity in these regions. Many estates were confiscated, land pillaged and populations terrorised. Perhaps the most spectacular event of this type was the seizure of Illésházy's land and his branding as a traitor. Illésházy, Thurzó, Istvánffy and the others all take their proper places in Hankiss' vivid narrative.

The brutality of Rudolf's commanders in Transylvania led István Bocskay, once a devoted supporter of the Hapsburgs, to retaliate by raising an army (called the *Hajduks*) against the Emperor. He drove the Imperial army out of Transylvania and Upper Northern Hungary, everywhere garnering popular support. In 1606 he concluded the Peace of Vienna with Emperor Rudolf.

This left him prince during his lifetime of an enlarged Transylvania and guaranteed the rights of the Protestants in Hapsburg Hungary. Bocskay also mediated the Peace of Zsitvatorok at the end of that year, between the Porte and the Emperor. This unburdened the Hapsburgs of their tribute to the Sultan, but left the territorial partition unaltered. Bocskay died a few weeks later. Poison was rumoured, and the usual struggle for power followed.

Hankiss' "History Lessons" reveal a country that has been divided, overrun and subject to foreign tyranny through centuries, and which has produced factions and conspiracies of Byzantine complexity. The author allows, even emphasises, resonances across the centuries and at times reduces historical figures to type, for example by pointing up the similarity between the Renaissance Bishop Szuhay and later Archbishop Szelepcsényi, whose actions echoed each other though they served different masters and lived in different centuries. Thus Hankiss exposes the "romance" of Hungarian history as essentially a circle of deceit. This motif cuts across both narratives and highlights the "real" romance of Susanna and her personal triumphs and tragedies. Here the historical events are merely the subtext of the story of a woman's journey to eventual self-enlightenment.

Hankiss' intention is further signalled by her references in the novel to Elizabeth Báthory, a noblewoman of the Transylvanian ruling family who has been mythologised as the original vampire, because of her purported habit of bathing in the blood of young girls, and whose crimes were probably distorted during the numerous witch hunts pursued by the Catholics between 1610 and 1630. This should remind us that women have to write their own stories if they are to become truly visible.

Emma Roper-Evans

A Hungarian Romance

Johann Kaspar Lavater:
What is the depth of your knowledge?

Cagliostro (in short):
In words, in the grass, and in rocks.

1

The exceptionally beautiful Susanna Forgách was born in the ancient castle of Komjáti on the first of January, 1582. Here King Mátyás had once danced, carousing for seven nights under its low sloping arches and gently rounded vaults, by its chill, crumbling walls and squat columns. He was, of course, strictly *incognito* (that is, until his farewells).

As a child Susanna had learnt about the dim and distant events of the royal visit from the end of a rambling, anxious, after-dinner conversation between her father, Imre, and his younger cousin, Bishop Ferenc Forgách. She had taken refuge under the great dining table and was hidden beneath its floor-length brocade table cloth, which crackled and rustled as if woven from autumn leaves and light footfalls. She crouched down, her chin on her knees, and listened. After some time she discovered to her delight that, although she was shrouded in darkness, the flowing words and rich silences wheeling above her head revealed to her the very stuff of life, its dormant fires and mysteries.

But even so she found the conversation somewhat boring.

It was no accident that the king's name had been mentioned; it was constantly on their lips, always accompanied by sighs and lamentations. It was often alluded to because Mátyás was also the name of the cold and ambitious younger brother of the then ruling, mad Emperor Rudolf, offspring of a decaying, sadistic and deformed dynasty. Each was a sad counterpart to the other: one embodied the independent Hungary of the past, the other, the present Hapsburg Hungary. They referred to them privately as "Big Mátyás" and "Little Mátyás". It was against this background, filled with suffering and longing, that the conversation took place.

Imagine the great king: a slight twist of his neck (a loose button or frayed thread would have ruined everything) and the shabby travelling cloak slipped from his shoulders and fell like a bag of shot game onto the dust of the courtyard. There Mátyás stood in all his royal finery, in a light summer shirt made from gossamer-white muslin, interwoven with geometric stars of golden thread, its folds and pleats stretched taut across his strong, muscular shoulders. The shirt was crumpled and his hair, usually so carefully combed and curled, fell in dishevelled ringlets as he threw off his soldier's cap, but it made no difference to his regal bearing. (Later his servant would remove the tell-tale bits of fluff from his back... He trailed behind the king carrying all the necessary royal paraphernalia crammed into a portmanteau.) Beneath the felt hat, which someone retrieved as if it were a runaway child and then laid gingerly on the cloak, Mátyás wore a garland of flowers made from precious stones as irridescent as the sheen on a butterfly's wing. His familiar face, full of adolescent charm, became a little drawn as the playful farce unfolded before him on that close, humid summer morning. He held a hurried audience and listened with gracious patience to the complaints, grievances and problems, true and false, of those assembled gaping at his feet. His responses were ready (*rex ex machina*), and he distributed money and even his own clothes to the poorest, a very model of charity.

The three Forgách daughters had known about that final scene of the royal visit since their early childhood, as virtually all those living in the castle had stories of a great-great-grandfather or mother who had received a gift, even those who had only recently come to the country. But the prudish chroniclers had not touched upon the events that occurred between the masked arrival and the self-revealing farewell; the seven nights of celebrations, of revelling and feasting and its painful consequences! Or perhaps it was not the chroniclers who were prim but the chronicles; it is usually that way, is it not?

In any case it was this interlude that was now being discussed above Susanna's head. Her father and cousin were debating with great gravity (they were actually enjoying themselves) the true purpose of this legendary, disguised visit.

They agreed that the final beneficent scene was merely a facade, that it had a hidden meaning.

Why had a disguise been necessary to discover what was happening in the country? Did not the deluge of problems and complaints that reached the court reveal enough?

How could a crowned ruler have set out on a masquerade around the country without proper escort? Or perhaps his retinue had all been in disguise as well...?

Is it possible that a mere hat, whether cowl or helmet, could really have concealed the face that gazed out from so many paintings and was stamped on every coin? What contrived, stumbling speech could mask that refined and cultivated voice in boorish accents?

To come to the point: the whole affair must have been carefully staged and prepared down to the last detail.

"I do not envy those who were honoured by a visit," remarked Bishop Forgách with an unaccustomed smile. The bishop had an ageless face, its supple rigour that of a man who awaited a great future, although occasionally he could appear generous, even cheerful (as if the sun had burst through the clouds for a moment).

Suppose they had received the masked ruler as if he

really had been a simple peasant or wandering soldier (there would of course have been much preparation before his arrival, but we will not dwell on this now), the charge of high treason would have hung like the Sword of Damocles above their heads. Alternatively, if he had been received in a more conventional way, without ritual but with careful delicacy and respect, they would have deprived him of something. Unless of course they were people of low cunning and guile - but how could they have been? After all, they were not brought up in a pedlar's kitchen! And deprived him of what? The pleasure of the game? The question is, what pleasure did the king derive from his disguise?

"Do you understand what I am talking about?"

Imre Forgách understood and smiled. The bishop would have continued anyway, even if his cousin had not; he was a very determined man.

Finally, after much soul-searching, they decided that there were only two possible explanations for the king's behaviour - desire for love or desire for power - but which, we shall never know.

It is possible (explanation number one) that the king found pleasure in the disguise itself: the desire to plunge into a secret, masochistic adventure, to taste a new experience, to wallow in the heady magic of self-abasement...the pleasure of stolen, casual loves which are at once the sweetest and the most confining. All this could be assuaged only by an act of charity.

But it is also possible (explanation number two) that the king had enjoyed not the mask, but the shedding of it: the moment of self-revelation, its wizardry, when the feeling of omnipotence bursts from the depths of the soul with the elemental force of a welling spring. He who possesses temporal power can also feel divine. If this is so, the sudden revelation of omnipotence was essentially part of the game, dazzling us like the sun.

However, we must not be overcome with veneration, for the discreet (or not so discreet) emanations of limitless power can be evil. Both were well aware of this. Mad Rudolf's moony face hung in the air around them; it pervaded the land like fog, they could not forget it.

"It's the oldest trick in the world," said Imre Forgách, breaking his pensive silence. He was slightly in awe and a little jealous of his cousin's worldly wit and religious profundity. "Just think of the archangel who approached the sleeping Noah in the guise of a poor vagabond."

In turn Ferenc Forgách spoke of Zeus who ravished Europa by taking the form of a white bull (referring to the first explanation). And so they looked to theology, to mythology, to ethical and spiritual interpretations.

At this point Susanna fell asleep under the table, but the secrets hidden in the words hummed and buzzed in her head. The conversation had intrigued her, it awoke in her a wild curiosity to explore the deepest labyrinths of creation.

Later she was to read a lot about *Mathias Rex Hungaria*, and he was to fire her imagination for years to come.

She pictured him as an isolated man of thorns, a man who became bitter and callous, an impulsive creature who travelled over wild lonely marshes like a will-o'-the-wisp. She wanted to be the only one to see behind his lonely mask, the one for whom he yearned, for whom he would leave his demanding Italian queen - that poor woman who bathed in magical, murky brews from dawn to dusk to get herself with child. To Susanna he would come disguised, and she would extend warm hands of greeting, bursting like the shining chestnut out of its wet shell...

She imagined him playing hide and seek, leaping out from behind doors and laughing at her. For her he would throw off his regal dignity and toss it into her lap. She made up absurd fantasies about him but always came back to earth with a jolt. After all, what can one do with a man who is not only a king, but has been dead for over a century?

2

Life in the castle went on. The father, Imre Forgách, in his melancholic, widowed solitude, often did not stir from his room for days. He just sat like a hermit watching the sun or the burning candles slowly dropping wax. If one burnt out, he lit another - in this way all was spent. Or so it appeared to his daughters and visitors.

He had many visitors. Female relations and women of the area, chiefly widows, often came; on tiptoe they approached, gently opening the door, bringing comfort and presents, and finding him like sorrow seated on a tomb. Their sweet prey would just pick at the offered delicacies, at the fresh fruit in covered baskets, and protest he did not deserve such kindness, truly he did not... So that they clucked over his small appetite, staring deeply into his tear-clouded, waiting eyes. He accepted everything gratefully, thanked them in a voice soft as velvet and ... nothing more.

But sooner or later the daughters needed a mother to bring them up. Klara Soós Poltári was a distant relation and had been a close friend of the girls' mother (the late Katalin Zrínyi, who had combined all the charm and clumsiness of a kitten). Klara's round, smiling face was both gentle and mischievous; her short figure billowed and curved. Her hands smelled of sweet milk, hot fat and raw onions. This mixture was so deep in her pores that it remained even after scrubbing.

"Dear, kind Klara! I know that for a woman full of life like yourself it is not the kindest gift of fate to come under the same roof as a gloomy, sick old man whose unavoidable misfortunes have mistreated him so, that he derives more pleasure from his solitary, domestic life than he could extract from the whole of society. And so I ask you with the greatest respect and highest esteem to take on the responsibility of cultivating my daughters and controlling them. For this you are assured of the humble but comfortable existence which my house offers, sweet, kind Klara!"

On reading this, Klara burst into tears. Then she wiped them away and called her friends together. Her friends thoroughly examined the meaning of each word and sentence; Klara, after every reading, carefully folded the letter, patted it as if it were an ironed sheet, but with slightly trembling hands. Finally (could it have been otherwise?) the blushing convocation decided unanimously that what lay before them (whether spread out or folded up, no matter) was nothing more than an old-fashioned proposal of marriage in a most discreet and tactful form. Thus Klara reviewed her wardrobe (mending over the holes with tiny flowers, crocheting this and that, embroidering collars), placed her belongings in a cart and soon arrived at Komját.

But on the first evening it became apparent that her host's behaviour, though charming, was distant. It seemed there were to be no autumn celebrations, no second blooming. Instead of a soft touch, there was a firm hand-shake; instead of tender looks, he expected bustling practicality from the wishful Klara. And his smile! That smile, like a peaceful island rising above lashing waves, which earlier - when Klara had come as a visitor - had warmed her in his discreet and searching gaze, as if he thought of her as his sister and partner, now - it was impossible not to notice - his eyes avoided her, his smile was fixed, nothing more.

And the rhythm of their relations had also changed. Before, all his gestures had been ceremonious, radiating dignity...as if he held something back, as if he were mulling over something in his movements and words. Now, however, things had changed drastically - as if his clipped, off-hand manner were intended to crush all the desires he had stirred.

Imre Forgách showed Klara her future room, rather like a hurried porter, polite, but going no further than the threshold. Klara still hoped that this would be only until the announcement of the wedding. But later they sat opposite each other, and the man revealed to her very honestly the state of war existing between his daughters - in particular between the eldest, Maria, and the youngest, Susanna, who were like fire and water, cat and dog. Klara's whole being shivered as she tried with all her strength to suppress the flood of injured feelings. In vain. She tried to listen to his words, but the velvety voice, the gentle implication of his superiority that surged through the conversation encircled and exhausted her. Even so, she nodded eagerly. Later she tried a trivial experiment. This happened after supper. When Imre Forgách wished her good night ("I hope, dear Klara, that everything is to your satisfaction"), she stared at the man again - a blue-water lake covered with grey fog could not have been more hopeless - and softly remarked (whispered? casually stated?) that she would never give him up... Imre Forgách's impatience could be distinguished behind his soft (too soft) sigh, so that Klara quickly withdrew her eyes from the man's beautifully-turned profile, and the sentence remained unsaid (or perhaps such sentences are impossible to finish). She blew her nose ("It seems I have caught a cold"), and settled for good at Komjáti.

For a time she wept, mostly at night.

Imre Forgách, however, travelled more and more frequently. When he started to prepare (packing trunks and harnessing horses), Klara would stand before him - always at the last minute - and ask with alarm and wonder, as if the question was more than rhetorical: "So you are going away again?" Was he annoyed? apologetic? pitiful? (certainly!) He always replied that he had to go on business to Trencsén... There was some truth in this, as Imre Forgách had tried several times to acquire Trencsén Castle.

In his absence, when anybody called on him, whether acquaintance or stranger, Klara would declare knowingly and severely that the master of the house had had to go to Trencsén on business, as if she knew precisely what that meant. But the truth was that these three words, so easy to say, "Trencsén on business", slowly lost any ordinary meaning they might have had and took on a higher significance, a life of their own. They carved in Klara's soul a vast, rich empire. They took over her life, whatever its outward bustle of activity. They were the song of the songbird in her tower-room cage, the mantra of her day-dreams. So longing and jealousy filled the muddy riverbed up to its stony banks.

3

Klara looked after the girls just as she patched up holes with her odds and ends. She jealously guarded them from the cold and the heat, from too much and too little; she always called them my Mariska, my Iluska, my Susaka - never anything else; she looked after their clothes, she sighed over them, tied ribbons in their hair; and they didn't thank her for any of it, that was the best thing about it. She was grateful if the girls called her mother; even if she perceived their mild contempt (primarily from Maria), she did not allow it into her heart ("...because one must only see good in people, only good!")

She oversaw every practical activity that the season dictated; needlework, horticulture and so on were done under her command. She disdained the higher issues of moral conduct, the higher dilemmas, however, leaving them to Imre Forgách with the same tacit understanding, the same peremptory wish to be left alone that he had tried to convey to her. So that father and nurse played a mutual, unspoken game of pass the parcel - the Forgách girls meanwhile spending their childhood in relative freedom. At times the adults would retire for three days, and private regrets would stream forth like ribbons on a Maypole, despite the fact that neither of them ever complained openly about their problems.

Only the silence betrayed them, like a forgotten glove, something left behind, revealing that disappointed people lived here.

4

The Forgách girls partook of two catechisms, one conducted by long-bearded Catholic priests, the other by clean-shaven missionary pastors. At first they alternated daily between the Catholics and the Protestants; but the teachers soon became intimate with each other (the Counter-Reformation was only then being conceived in the heads of the crowned and the mitred). They sat

together around the fireplace or in the shade of a nut
tree in the society of their disciples, who listened with
large eyes and giggled to hear the cross-fire of theological
controversies, the clash of dogmas, prayers and Psalters
dancing a *pas de deux*. The girls' spirits were captivated
by David and Moses, saints and apostles in turn. They
mocked them, they tickled the soles of King David's feet
while Saint Cecilia's moonlight violin solo amused them;
they made fun of her supplications, of her pained
staccato; they were frivolous about the Psalter; they
pulled Moses' saintly beard and worked out their own
Ten Commandments. The priests and pastors enjoyed
themselves hugely, especially as Klara sent them freshly
baked cakes. The priests brought gifts of holy medallions,
which they flourished ostentatiously, especially when
there was an afternoon sitting with their Reform
colleagues (most delightful!). The girls loved the minia-
tures, they wondered and commented on The Virgin's
silks and Saint Elizabeth's fine veil. Susanna would turn
her head away as she returned to its case the one of
Saint Sebastian with his thousand open wounds, quivering with arrows and writhing in coagulated blood. (For a
time it caused her certain pangs of conscience.)

5

Even a perfect stranger could see that Susanna was Imre
Forgách's favourite, though no one ever mentioned it. By
contrast Maria, before she was allowed in the door,
before she could pour him a drink, had to lay out the
soft, red carpet. However, in the girls' arguments
(frequent) it was with Maria that their father agreed as

far as possible.

The struggle between Maria and Susanna was not so much something palpable as an occasional subterfuge. The reasons for it were not apparent, as the sisters were actually very like each other.

But the tiny differences covered by this "actually" meant that so much about their lives were different, all the thorns and hobgoblins of personality came between them. Both were blonde, but while one, Susanna, was like golden rain, flowing honey, a bright clearing in a virgin forest; Maria had the unkempt straw of a suffering Christ. The colour of their eyes was also similar; but whereas one had eyes like green meadows in the sunshine, the other's were like the dingy water in which Klara had dyed her dress before she moved to Komjáti.

Susanna never mislaid anything: glasses, books, scissors - all were in order. But if Maria even attempted to hang something up, then the object would just as promptly fall down, as out would come its nail with an indiscreet thump. Susanna's drawers were crammed with all sorts of useful odds and ends, but Maria could never find anything when she needed it.

Susanna would take great bites out of the bread, the jam or honey running down her chin; this is how she started the day. Maria breakfasted only towards noon, if at all.

Susanna slept deeply, without stirring. For Maria, the wind might blow her curtains, and she would see black spiders descending onto her covers.

The middle Forgách daughter, Ilona, was a brunette with brown eyes, pleasing, but not particularly good-looking. She was eternally struggling like a small, wild animal in the trap of the other two, caught between the favourite and the bully. She was torn between Maria's complaints that Susanna was free to do whatever she liked, and Susanna's, that Maria would even restrict the grass from blowing in the wind because her whole being was made of nothing but bitterness and overblown pride... (indeed, even the priests were chastised by Maria). Ilona gave her heart to Susanna - all the signs in daily pleasures and games pointed to this - but at the end of the day she submitted to Maria's arrogance encased in its fine skein of tact.

There were often storms at Komjáti, stirred from defections, contradictions and resentments among the sisters, usually ending with Susanna calling Ilona a little toady, she (Ilona) making excuses, well yes, yes, and poor Maria would become ill again...

Because Maria Forgách was often ill. Heartburn, giddiness... An over-sensitive body was definitely a part of her self-immolating, self-pitying selfishness. This was the triangle with which Maria framed herself in her dreary, joyless life; she juggled with these three *s*'s most skilfully.

She would exhale a wreath of silent reproaches even if she didn't complain or accuse anyone. She collected false injuries, all sorts of trivial happenings. Her fountain of pretences was truly a horn of plenty; the family could only observe and catalogue them, saying to each other that Maria was unable to take on anything other than her own problems. She could make the losing of a pretty button into a huge scandal. And if there was a decision to be made about her appearance, whether blue or grey looked better with her dun-coloured hair or suited her pale, devout face, then she would firmly decide that for the next family meal she would change to the opposite.

Because she always had a plan in mind.

Her one aim was to protect her obstinate uniqueness, to exhibit her pampered, aristocratic ways. She played this affected role in every endeavour... Nobody could influence so much (usually drastically) the family's daily mood, as she. And when she lay behind closed doors with a cold compress laid to her heart's feverish beat, it was then that she reigned supreme.

So everyone had to look for the button.

Klara arrived on the scene, but Maria stopped her from clattering the furniture about. While Klara stood hesitating, Maria said in a quavering voice that that blouse with the missing button was the only one she liked... And when the button did not turn up, she was insufferable at the next meal. When Maria sulked, she seemed to accuse the glasses, the linen table cloth, and even her father, who could least bear it, and who, over the injured party's ostentatious protests, offered to send messengers to Pozsony or even to Prague to replace the missing button. When Klara (who loathed all unnecessary exhibitions) and Susanna (who did too) offered to make another one, Maria immediately thanked them, but said that all the proper shades had run out, and black did not go with blue, only brown - everyone knew that. They had grown into the habit of imagining that Maria alone knew what suited, what was beautiful and what was ugly. Although sometimes - if she was in a reasonable mood, or had by chance been cornered - she might append an "at least I think so". This was merely an addendum, and a moment of constraint did not mean that her usual calculating behaviour would change.

Thus when the mounted errand boy returned from his dangerous journey (for the roads in those days were dangerous in every respect) with the yearned-for button, radiating all the glitter and fashion of the Imperial Court, Maria merely gave it a passing and superficial glance. Her look strayed to the secret distance of the garden, to the white blossoming branches there, as if she could have no need of fashion's ornaments! Then her gestures grew lofty and brittle, the princess of a sham ivory tower.

Imre Forgách, poor man, started to remonstrate, but mumbling about joy to a joyless, haggling martyr was futile. She had got her way. Who could imagine that for her, Maria Forgách, who filled every free minute with the reading of holy texts and important domestic tasks (because who else, after all, could be trusted with them?), that for her the possession of a mere button could take on such proportions; it was outrageous, laughable!

Maria eagerly took on tasks and obligations. So she lashed herself to the mast of duty with the countless welts of compulsory acts and lofty examples. Because her destiny took a circuitous route, she persistently blamed the world - in fact the world was to disprove her reproaches and accusations in a thousand and one ways...

Hence the existence of two stubbornly opposed natures, two variants in perpetual conflict with each other. One Forgách daughter the favourite, best suited to narcissism and idle pleasures (though the possibility of amorous conquest was also open to her...). The other, rebellion cloaked in injury, the moral merchant whose loftiness was her revenge.

Was it so simple?

No, it was not. (Favourites suffer great falls, as we know even without singling out the archetypal Joseph of the Old Testament or other spectacular examples, with the heavens and hells of their reconciliations and triumphs.)

It is both simple and not so simple. But for the time being, it is still simple...

And yet it can never be simple in this reversible garment (which if I want can seem perfectly clean-cut, even monotonous, or if I want can seem darkly swathed and inexplicable), this magic coat that clothes the human soul.

6

Wandering soldiers (Hungarians) and billeted Germans often turned up at the castle. The soldiers told stories about - what else? - the many different kinds of death, about the cruelty of the Turks and Germans, kidnapping, starvation, massacre, poverty and fratricide. These accounts drew before the girls' eyes all the suffering and injuries of the past century (to be repeated with just as much devastation in the impending one). They naturally shivered and cried, so that Klara, fearing illness, would keep them indoors. Then they would hide away, wrapping themselves up in their curtained cocoon.

The soldiers came and went. But one of them, Cyprian Virgil Basirius, stayed on at Komját, and for a small monthly sum became the court musician.

In place of one eye he had an opalescent glass one, but otherwise he had a beautiful face reminiscent of Greek sculptures, softly framed by curls.

Discovering anything about his previous life and occupations was not easy, or at least nothing was certain. Although he often and eagerly talked about himself, he said something a little different each time - but so naturally, it seemed his biography was a white sheet, a clean white sheet.

He said, for example, that the Turks had kidnapped his mother and taken her straight to the Sultan's harem, where she had lived ever since, her face still beautiful, but very fat, because she distributed favours and titles from a sugar box. Even so, she had not forgotten her son: every full moon she sent him wonderful *mufti* with the help of a disguised Turk. Nobody had ever heard of this word, was it Turkish, perhaps? But he only ever said *mufti* and clicked his tongue and promised that he would show it. Sometimes he talked as if it was some type of clothing, another time as if it was an object you were not allowed to open, but that he had opened nevertheless. One sad, rainy day he said that his mother, poor thing, had been killed in her room by a stray bolt of lightning just as she was rocking him in her arms... When she heard this, Klara gently said that this must surely have happened in Constantinople? But he immediately said that was only his stepmother... and just smiled.

When he smiled, his white teeth gleamed as if life's most alluring secrets were shut together behind a grilled gate that anyone could slip through.

Maria openly hated the musician. "That Cyprian, he's just a vagabond, idly boasting at every word. And those little secrets he twists round his fingertips as if they were precious jewels are only worthless bottle-tops thieved from here and there. Mark me, he only stays with us because there's tender meat to be had, that's for sure!"

By contrast Susanna soon became friends with the musician. In great secret she showed him her first - strictly religious - poems (tender, psalm-like plants). But Cyprian just glanced through them and declared they were atrocious (perhaps he was right). What was done was done, but there was still the music. Susanna became his most devoted pupil; she was soon playing several instruments and singing so beautifully that even Cyprian Virgil Basirius had to acknowledge her.

Sometimes (if no one was looking) he would sit Susanna on his knee, put his arms round her and place his hands delicately on the strings (later he would get bolder).

He taught her to play on the virginals and the flute, linking the roaming hands of a Palm Sunday with the discovered senses of all the burning hymns and mysteries. This usually took place in the semi-darkness of the knights' hall amidst the rusting-stiff armour which was hung in hilarious or fearful poses, among the displayed weapons. Susanna fidgeted and wriggled in the musician's lap, put her hand on his shoulder and drank up the smell of his hair, his skin, his cloak... Cyprian Virgil Basirius always smelled of rain. Even when there had been none. It was like the smell after a summer shower when the sun, without warning, comes out from behind the clouds and the ground steams with a gentle fragrance... or perhaps it was the damp walls? (Everything in the hall was always dank and mouldy; it was here the passing soldiers were lodged; the place was not heated for them, so to give an impression of their host's austerity.) She could also smell that fragrance on the young man's face and on the curve of his neck as they wandered freely through the tall grass of the garden, among its flowering branches and luxuriant trailing ivy.

But the indoor trysts and outdoor wanderings soon came to an end (at the best time or the worst? it depends on your point of view...). It happened like this: one day Maria - who had become more and more suspicious of these extra lessons, feeling that her sister's industry was not at all characteristic - hurried after them to the knights' hall. She peeped around the door that was ajar, and what she saw (what she was forced to see) awakened a great storm in her soul... She would have run to their father with her treasure of unwelcome news, but Imre Forgách was at that moment away on "Trencsén business".

So she ran to the family priest. She trampled the dust of the courtyard and ran through the chapel as if the devil himself was after her. Such a wild and greedy impatience thundered inside her that she was incapable of bothering with etiquette or a stealthy entrance. She simply burst in on the Father and hurled angry sentences at him like a coarse warder shouting at a prisoner. That was not the worst of it. When she finally started her story, she went right back to the Flood. (And even that was perhaps *in media res*? The question is, where does one look for the core of things, on the inside, or on the outside?) Hidden behind her words was the indescribable depth of her hatred for her sister, which for so long she had felt inwardly, but could now say out loud... balm for the convulsions of her soul.

At first the priest was not really aware of Maria's desires and agitations.

He was indeed rather bored by her ramblings; his eyelids drooped lower and lower. He realised what Maria was there for only when she finally recounted the scene in the hall; and only when, in her minutely detailed version, she reached the moment when Susanna's blonde hair, as soft as the naked Magdalen's, spread over the musician's slender, angular shoulder. Then did the priest finally listen. With splutters and stutters Maria went on about that lesson, that lesson, how they were stroking each other's hands in the most shameless manner under the musician's cloak. The priest then spoke for the first time: Had Susanna slipped off her ring?

Maria stood amazed. She had not really noticed and, with a slightly idiotic, inquiring look at her own ring of precious stones, said this was not important and returned to her seething moral chant... Finally she unwisely confessed (a struggle for the crown) that what she really wanted was the death of her younger sister, and not once only, nor in one way.

The priest no longer seemed to be paying attention.

However, the following day at dawn Cyprian Virgil Basirius left Komját... *sans adieux*.

Susanna wept, but not for very long. Fortunately she was of a cheerful disposition.

7

Maria was the first to be married off. One day Peter Révay, his mother and younger brother arrived at Komjáti.

Lady Mihaly Révay was a commanding character, although she never issued an order. Before her, dogs came to heel and the dying commenced to die, as if she were connected to all the woes and sorrows of the world. Behind her gentleness and her simple kindness, she was as hard as steel. For her a plank of wood was a plank of wood, whether it was used to build a scaffold or a carved cupboard door...

Klara did not perceive this because she was so upset (and at the same time weakened) by the wedding plans, which worried and goaded her most private thoughts. She was scared, as small children are before a sleeping adult, but with the same unwavering obduracy.

Thus, after their elders had left the young couple in an awkwardly ceremonial way to begin to get acquainted, Klara immediately began ("I don't really know why this came to mind"), saying that Imre Forgách needed a wife, a suitable wife. The guest merely looked at her and smiled and nodded. Klara, however, continued in an intimate, droning way that he should get married soon... If he didn't go to the altar, he would go to his grave...

They almost forgot about the young people. But when the two of them had finally made their intentions clear to each other with small blushes and protests, they sighed with relief. Though in her father's presence Maria had kept her mouth pursed as if in suffering, to her suitor she quickly volunteered that she had no objection to the marriage. The truth was that she found Peter Révay fairly attractive; he stood about confusedly, with an open look and with a certain guileless calm. He had a smiling, chubby face framed by ringlets, and the down on his skin was like a ripe peach. Maria herself shimmered. She was a glorious sight, beautifully dressed as she was for the occasion, her long, slim neck framed by the weight of her hair. She was like a candle sitting on a birthday cake.

(But do not forget that marriage was a business transaction, with all its thrilling absurdity, though the spirit of the age - for a good while yet - would try to keep this hidden.)

Maria often wrote to her father.

The marriage made her calmer and less bitter - and the change entailed plans, difficulties and small triumphs. At times she could forget her tragedies on the following day; but sometimes she mulled over old anxieties for weeks, ranting and raving about the most banal things.

8

They also married Ilona off. She moved a good distance away. Imre Forgách, however, kept repeating that, before he was summoned from the world of shadows into the world of light, he would like to know that all his girls were safe.

Even the youngest one.

So much the more because Maria kept raising the idea in her letters that they marry her younger sister to the youngest Révay boy. Maria was never at a loss to praise Ferenc Révay's "moral gravity", or at another time his "grave morality". She dwelt at length on the familial and financial advantages of the marriage. Such dove-like gentleness and goodwill she had never displayed at Komjáti with all her door banging and damp compresses.

"Well, well, how time heals!" (Klara).

Imre Forgách remembered Ferenc Révay well. It was not difficult to recall him, with his smooth pale face, his tall figure, his thin hair and his strange, inward-burning obstinacy. Forgách was scandalised that this doleful cold fish, fresh from the seminary, should become lord and master over his exceptionally beautiful daughter. At other times when he heard about Ferenc Révay's seriousness and level-headedness, he believed he could see true wisdom behind the young man's silent obduracy. Then he would meditate over the Révays' great prestige and even greater wealth, over their grand, cliff-top castle, over their fine educations and fine leather books...

One day he took Susanna by the hand and led her to his tower room, up the creaking, narrow stairs into his secret male sanctuary.

The hooped iron lock on the cupboard door could be opened only with special keys. The girls had always believed that their father kept his Trencsén business letters in there.

But look! It was only his dead wife's old clothes, which he, Imre Forgách, had wanted to show Susanna, to her alone.

There were all sorts of garments: a wedding veil of snowflake lace, her white honeymoon blouse carefully ironed, her parturition dress clotted red, her expectant, sorrowful brown shawl, her agonising alabaster handkerchief crumpled up in a ball; pressed flowers and artificial ones, souvenirs of a long walk or a carnival, Turkish patterned fans, presents brought by passing visitors; a tiny bag with pearl beads instead of pin-prick stitches. The colours whirled and eddied, and in Susanna's eyes every colour represented a phase of life. All pressed together between crumpled lavender, so that you had to shake the tiny seeds out of every garment.

"You must tidy them away."

"I will ask Klara."

But Imre Forgách did not want Klara to touch the clothes.

"Klara was a good friend of my mother's."

Even so. Somehow even so...

As Susanna shook out and folded the things, a little overcome, her father gently told her that they two, he and Katalin Zrínyi, would often hide here if they wanted to be alone.

"She had terribly thin wrists - Maria is most like her. Perhaps due to her over-sensitivity, her hands were often sore if she sewed or read much. Then I would take her hand and stroke it. I would clasp her wrists tightly and then suddenly release them; she loved that. Sometimes I was afraid that her bones would break, but she laughed and said that even so, I must clasp them more bravely..."

Susanna put down the clothes and listened. Now she was seriously touched. It seemed that a marriage really could be like this..., and she greedily awaited the rest.

But all of this was only the preface and introduction to more important news.

It was as if he had raised her up to great heights with one hand only to push her down with the other.

9

He was a soft-spoken man, a man with burning eyes, inwardly burning. A smooth yet ungainly man, a gawky yet veiled man, the son of a frightening woman, of a hard, upright character (who had since luckily died). A silent man who, once he started to speak, would go on to the end of what he had to say with extraordinary deliberation and precision, as if he could not let go.

She would perhaps have accepted him gladly as an elder brother.

It was as if he was continually measuring people up, studying them at his leisure. His eyes flickered like fugitives. He hardly ever sat down, but rather remained standing.

She, Susanna, just sat, her hands dropped in her lap, wishing she could soar away into the air.

A puzzling man who, if he looked at her, at Susanna, did it surreptitiously, as if his gaze would set alight her skirt or blouse.

She touched his elbow, slipped an icicle into his palm, blew a dandelion in his face, in the hope of getting to know this man who was after all to be her husband.

He shook it all off, as a delicate pedigree dog shakes off muddy water.

If only she could fly away.

She looked around her. Clothes being sewn and bed linen ironed with feverish excitement. Embroidering, weaving, stitching, folding. The goods piled up suffocatingly. The trunks bulged, the wardrobes stood empty. Empty shelves, empty room, empty soul, empty sky.

Sometimes even she fell under the spell of preparation, and jostled and threw things about; for it was a good feeling to be preparing. The high clouds of adult life descending with beckoning arms, this too was alluring.

The rest just frightened her. If only she could fly away.

Susanna Forgách married Ferenc Révay in 1598. On the twenty-first of April they sat at a great feast under decorated canopies which were swelled, stretched and snapped by the wind. As the tent-poles shifted, up went great cries of Oh God, Dear Jesus, it's going to come crashing down on the tables groaning with all those delicacies. (This did in fact happen later, but by then everyone was sated, so no one minded...) They sang and danced, they organised races of foamy-mouthed white horses along the bank of the rising river between the flowering trees. Fleecy clouds, starry sky, plenty of guests and presents - there was everything that there should be.

It was only among the patted and plumped lace pillows and soft silk covers that all did not go as every staggering guest confidently expected and jocularly hinted at.

Ferenc Révay became ill. Was his stomach upset? Was the sudden warm spell too much for him? One could only guess. In any case, until the first glimmers of dawn Susanna Forgách was brewing, then cooling soothing teas (it was no mean task to find the right temperature), changing compresses, opening windows and closing them again as the sick man shivered or flushed. For a long time the din of the revelry filtered in from the garden, a chorus of the last tired hurrahs; towards dawn those awake and those with hangovers greeted one another raucously in the corridors. Inside the wedding chamber, the sick-room where Susanna Forgách had, with some-what mixed feelings, nursed her husband, they heard the same words over and over (one couldn't for a moment doubt their spicy insinuations).

She now had very mixed feelings whenever she looked at him, at that stranger lying awake but with closed eyes before her. In his stubborn agonies glittered something mysteriously alluring (the life-long unravelling of a jigsaw puzzle...). His soft *thank-you*'s, when she changed his wet clothes or brought fresh tea, were incandescent. There glowed for a single, brief moment a hesitating, fumbling quest that pointed towards the cauldrons of wild passion or towards the icy grottoes of frightened concealment. It was as if he chose to be only a step away

from both. Meanwhile, he could not even sit up because
the room immediately started to spin; his forehead
throbbed, and perhaps he really was feverish...

10

One could gather a bouquet of the flowers of perdition
growing from the mire of early traumas and complexes.
But what for?

Let us confine ourselves here to saying that in every
respect Ferenc Révay had a most hesitant nature.

Before deciding anything, he thoroughly considered
the range of arguments and counter-arguments, pros and
cons. He shrank from all definite yeses and nos, and felt
secure only on the bridge between the two. If, however,
he did decide something because he had to, he felt
duped, defrauded and defenceless. Vague and exaggerated fears, rambling and raging passions tormented him.
To temporise and to regret: Ferenc Révay's life was
governed by these two until the last steps of the dance;
the act of linking them together swept over him, leaving
him confused and nauseated.

It was thus with his marriage, too.

When he caught sight of Susanna Forgách and noticed
(quite something for him) her rousing beauty, in those
confusing, awkward moments, he had felt as if life's most
dangerous forces were trifling with him. It was as if the
whole of Sweet God's siren chorus had at that moment
appeared right in front of his nose - their eyes downcast,
ergo most provocatively. He was afraid, he hemmed and
hawed. His dread sprang from the notion that Susanna
Forgách obviously could not love Ferenc Révay; not even

with the diluted, lukewarm love that grandmothers and wise old women call habit.

Before the wedding all three - the single Révay brother, the married one, and his wife - had lived in Holics Castle (which the brothers jointly owned).

On the second day of Christmas - when the mood tends once more to the routine, differentiating the last day of the feast from those before it, a day of anxious restlessness or its opposite, of unremitting relief, for some one, for some the other - Peter Révay could conceal it no longer. He was very tired of his wife's ceaseless arguments and all his brother's *yes-but* 's, stammerings and evasions, to the point where he could hardly wait to return to Vienna. They sat by the hearth; and, because they had no wish to speak to each other, they just stared at the fire, at the burning logs crumbling to ash. Maria especially liked this process, almost to obsession, the whole *grand guignol* of blazing and collapsing. Sometimes she would suddenly stand up to prod and stab the still glowing embers, then watch the effect. Her eyes lit up as if the transformations were entirely of her own doing.

Maria started to say once again, "If you took my sister, the family could at least stay together."

"Even then we might not stay here," said Ferenc, although it seemed likely because the Révay brothers, despite owning a good few castles in northern Hungary, had always lived under one roof. At this Peter raised his head and said with unusual firmness and irritation, "All right, let's forget the whole thing."

But Ferenc Révay would not suffer a categorical *no* either. His old doubts were replaced by new ones, like winds blowing in from opposite directions.

The following morning (Peter Révay was already on his way to Vienna) he knocked on Maria's door. Wrapped up in his fur coat against the cold, he lifted the latch hesitantly and politely, and stood in the doorway.

"I will get married."

Maria leapt from the bed and wound her long hair with astonishing speed around her head, securing it with a few hairpins snatched from beneath the pillow. Not very skilfully, because it soon all came loose, with the knot dangling on the upturned pins like a spinning top on its side. He could scarcely imagine what hand or wrath of God could hold her hair in place.

Maria embraced him and kissed him. She said he could not begin to imagine how happy he had made her. Taking him by the arm, she told him to come in quickly, sit down and they'd talk about everything in detail.

From the first, a deep and tacit understanding had grown between them. Not so much in words, more of a strong attraction which flowered in the empty corridor of each other's company. While Maria talked incessantly, planning or complaining, he generally just listened, and with Maria Forgách he felt calmer than he had ever done before.

But when the wedding day was announced, he panicked. He felt the decision had been rash; he watched the wedding preparations going on around him, but from the outside, almost as a stranger. And he dreamt of some convenient little illness or accident.

11

The castle of Szklabinya, where they went to live after the wedding, was built on the top of a small hill, in a trough screened by high mountains.

In the agonising weeks (months...) that followed the

mistaken wedding, Ferenc Révay reassured himself by
saying that he would do it tomorrow, or that one day is
nothing, but the truth was that every single day, every day
chalked up in the diary made crossing the threshold only
more difficult. When he thought about the "then...",
tingles and shivers welled up in his body - or rather his
torso. The weary acknowledgement of these familiar
feelings and their remote attraction would at another
time have been just that. But when he actually had to go
into the narrow, draughty corridor that separated their
bedchambers, it became a sort of invincible partition, a
shackling barrier which he had to struggle to break
through. His days were filled with a billowing despair that
burst against the walls like the dazed rituals of a broken-
winged bird, wild and self-damaging. To think of his
wife's sadness frightened him. It was the same to think of
her laughter.

A profound, remorseful silence reigned over the whole
house, a sluggish, weary stiffness. Apparent death within,
a smoothed facade without - this involved both of them.
For neither of them knew what to do. Thrown into a
state of paralysis, they were beached among the wreckage
of their collided fates.

Susanna felt the most extraordinary combination of
suffocation and relief, as if one would extinguish the
other.

Ferenc sometimes went to her (calmed by the creaks
and corridor noises...). But he just sat and tried to make
excuses, repeating in a veiled and awkward manner his
financial problems, the worrying news from abroad, and
his physical ill health. He released balloons of possible
reasons as if they had accidentally slipped out of his
hand; the lame record of possible explanations all came
to this, nothing more. But Susanna did not ask anything
from him. Relieved and desperate, she did not want this
marriage for real or for sham; but she did not know

which one she wanted least, the greater or lesser evil. She
did not know where to look for the cause; she did not
know which feeling - anger, shame, pity, resignation - all
now stirring and surging within her, should prevail. There
was nowhere to go to, no one to turn to; she just watched
him for signs of sympathy or rejection - but of course
found neither.

The words passed between them without friction, as if
the speakers were both there and not there. It was all
carefully managed so that nothing should obstruct the
gentle flow of tried and tested subjects.

As if he were her brother.

During this period their relations were terribly polite.
Indeed there reigned an amazing harmony. For instance,
neither wanted to leave the castle, to mix in society, to
travel or even to accept invitations.

However, from spring until autumn Susanna often
roamed round the garden and the nearby woods. (If she
stayed out too long, Ferenc sent someone to look for
her...)

She loved and knew by name the meadow and
woodland flowers. Particularly and quite precisely the
following: the tiny, white and purple sweet scabious
nestled among the high grasses on the sunny side of the
hills, and the long-stemmed, cone-shaped heliotropes,
whose teasels reminded her of fish scales, only denser.
On the marshy banks of the streams were spear-like
leaves. In their hollows rain drops collected (birds' wells)
and into these her fingertip just fit; she watched the
drops slide down and trickle on her finger, forming a
starry pool in her palm. She loved to touch the soft fluff
and chaff of the anemones, the delicate, filmy petals of
the poppies; but no matter how gently she treated them,
pieces would come off in her hand. Wild saffron, the
flower of ruin, the lily of doom, was also plentiful, as was
another straw-coloured flower with red threads in its

feathery centre, as if it were bleeding. This two-faced
flower was supposedly proffered to Charlemagne by an
angel to ward off the plague (for once two-facedness had
no sinister meaning... presumably). Clusters of cowslips,
cups and bells that seemed to want to break off; the
yellow-headed dandelions with their flowing milk and
flighty seeds; the small, sweet-smelling, moist fruit of the
wild strawberry; between the colourful berries and thorny
branches of the bushes, the just visible strands of a
delicate web, tangled with ancient mysteries. The light
tent of the pines, the prickly cases and the lustrous
treasured fruit of the wild chestnut; the intricate Jewish
candelabra of the cornflower, then another by the name
of Solomon's Seal, with big, pliant leaves like wind-blown
sheets hung out to dry, its flower like a white skirt with a
golden hem, the whole plant rich and luxuriant. She
could spot the woodland nettle too from afar, where its
roe-speckled leaves lit up the forest's darkness. The
frayed petals of Sweet William in worn velvet; the petals
of wild roses like butterflies - if she broke off a bloom
they'd be gone; the delights in the quivering grass; she
gazed at them all with devotion.

But the jam turned sour on her bread and her body
tossed in the night.

12

After Susanna had left home, Imre Forgách was pursued
by doubts, which in time forced him to conclude that
something was wrong with his daughter's marriage. For
the moment, though, this feeling fed on vague signs of

anguish, with no concrete evidence. Like a pause in the howling of distant dogs on winter dawns.

Moreover Klara's old hopes had revived since the last Forgách daughter had got married and left Komjáti. She chattered and twittered, feverishly dressing and doing herself up, so that Imre Forgách really had to avoid her.

Thus he was unable to share his misgivings with anyone.

Not even with his younger cousin, the great Ferenc Forgách.

Now the bishop (who was a vigorous supporter of the forces and advance of the Counter-Reformation) already disapproved of Maria Forgách's marriage to the Protestant Révay boy. Before Susanna's wedding he visited Imre Forgách and was even more persuasive than before, thrusting all the power and authority he could muster into his soaring eloquence, as he tried to stem new ideas and beliefs from entering the family. In any case rhetoric was the strongest side of the bishop's character. Written down, his words would have seemed wanner and wearier than what was spoken, perhaps because his rapacious nature needed the sight of live prey in palpable proximity for his intentions to blaze, his inspiration glow and his thoughts scald. The "razor of the pedagogue" - that's what they call it, isn't it? And it was true that, when he became acquainted not long after with Peter Pázmány, a young Jesuit, Ferenc immediately sensed that there was something hidden behind the young man's flair for eloquent debate: a latent and soaring surplus, an independent inspiration, precisely what was lacking from his own great "applied" knowledge. So he summoned the young Jesuit and offered him his summer residence as a quiet retreat, all would be provided, food and drink, only that he should not leave his room, and simply write and write and write.

But Imre Forgách was such a stranger to all religious

dogmas and matters of faith that instead of debating and defending himself, he usually just listened. He had only once ventured into this sphere when as a young man he had sent a letter to Catholic and Protestant (!) forums protesting against the introduction of the Gregorian Calendar... Strange. Or perhaps it was precisely the tendency to get things out of proportion that led to this out-of-character incident.

Now they sat in the library at the round table; Imre Forgách nervously twisted the tassels on the rustling-crackling cloth.

"This marriage could be very useful to us," he said finally, expressing his most intimate thoughts with astonishing openness, as twitches ran across his impassive face (like recurrent waves or those flickering tremors on a cat's spine before it leaps).

He who was normally so hesitant and reserved was now compelled to a vulgar and embarrassing openness. To state the harsh facts. But Ferenc Forgách dismissed it all with a wave of his hand.

Later Imre Forgách tried once again to appease the bishop by writing to him.

But he replied that in his view and opinion (what is the difference between the two?) a mixed marriage offends against the priesthood. He went on to cite the apostles and archangels.

To the wedding he simply sent a note wishing the young couple much happiness. Apostles and archangels alone knew what he understood by happiness.

13

Those misgivings that had briefly shunned Imre Forgách now returned to penetrate his self-protective layer and plague the sensitive man beneath.

He decided to write a letter to his son-in-law. This calmed him down.

"My dear boy, whom God has given me as a son, receive with a glad heart these lines from your respectful and loving father..."

He began a new page and composed afresh, "from your loving and respectful father..." - the final text became, "receive with a glad heart these lines from a father who wishes you well!" Then, after a few affable commonplaces as fluttery as muslin curtains, he carefully went on that Ferenc Révay's serious and moral nature might easily find fault with his extremely beautiful and perhaps over-lively daughter... His letter continued thus, "My dear son, do not act hastily and do something you might regret, first get to know her well, discover her hidden faults and ascertain your chances with loving patience. Whatever has happened or comes to pass, I beseech you to be understanding and forgiving in God's name!"

He ran through the letter, frowning. He feared that the most subtle essence of what he wanted to say might fall through the sieve of his noble expressions. So he added to the letter in a wholly different style, a completely exceptional postscript:

"If a mutual harmony grows between you, you are fortunate. You will be dear to both man and God. And happy. But if not, you will be the most unlucky man in this world. And the next. Your loving father."

14

Ferenc Révay was puzzled by the letter's opening. Why the affected salutation? A sign of discontent? A discontent related to "Whatever has happened..."? But when he got to the end of the letter, that arrogant addendum shocked him, it left a bad taste in his mouth.

He put the letter in his pocket, went out of the house into the garden and hid among the vine bowers. He withdrew, trembling inwardly, behind the curtain of luxuriant, curling vines which hung and scattered like violin clefs around him.

All the warmth of an Indian summer streamed in. It was decidedly pleasant. He was surrounded by sweet juice and sap, the table creaked to overflowing with grapes, their sticky skin and pulp coating its surface. Intoxicated wasps swarmed around him, but he was not scared of them. He was only scared of people. Besides, the wasps steered clear of his face during the sweeps and pivots of their death dance. Why did they circle so long above the grapes? He watched for a while their apparent restraint, their careful approach...and then their voracious surrender to greed.

He re-read the letter. On a second reading, the letter took on another aspect; all other possible barbs paled beside that dark word *happened*, with its poisoned sting hidden in the past tense ending, its brazen hyena laugh. From now on behind this past tense, in Ferenc's eyes, cowered mordant and wicked secrets; for inside him began to rage a mad carnival of suspicion. He read the letter for a third, fourth and fifth time, but the damage had been done: those clawing secrets would from now on grow fat and plunder the halls and dominions of his soul.

He brooded, he feverishly racked his memory; it occupied all his thoughts while he attended to his daily tasks, whether going about his estates or giving evidence in lawsuits in the various courts (the usual occupations of his rank).

He certainly did not demand explanations from his wife. He would not ask questions which might have precipitated an avalanche, the dropping of their mutual reserve. Rather, he determined with all his strength to transform the situation into something new.

To turn his shame into reproach... And that masterful seventh sense of his, which could allow no failing in himself, readily conjured up a wart-ridden world of deceit and disguise beneath the uneventful surface of things.

In the afternoon he lost his keys, in the evening he spilt ink on the table. If a meeting with his father-in-law was to come, he would be waiting for it.

15

Klara found Imre Forgách early one morning when she went into his room carrying the breakfast (this was Klara's one privilege and prerogative: with a soft and motherly "Good morning" to put down the tray, to draw the curtains, to rearrange the mussed covers).

At first glance he looked as if he were only sleeping. And of course for one who talks constantly about death like Imre Forgách, it is even more difficult to believe he has really died. After her first, uncheckable sobs abated, Klara kept repeating, "He could have had a beautiful life, poor man...," all the while clutching her fists. She looked down, as if the explanation was to be found there, hidden in the cracked bed of her nails. Then Klara set to work - beside the open coffin, among the be-ribboned and graceful tall candles and the delicate sanctuary lamps - to compose a final satisfactory chapter to the inner chronicle of her life. Her black lace veil clung to her mouth wet with tears, and with every huge sigh it bubbled out. The sobbing, the discreet splutter of the flames, the crumpled black silk of the bier, all this was enough to remind her that something else besides those things, some other tyranny of fate or trick of the Devil had thwarted her. That she, Klara Soós Poltári, could have been the last harbinger of joy to the deceased Imre Forgách. On the other hand, of course, this death was at least something of a victory over Trencsén.

But this small triumph did not last long. Everything was soon turned upside down. After the funeral Klara immediately set about sorting the remaining belongings and papers (which, to whom, what, to where). By evening her skin was dried out, and her lungs choked from the dust. And then, like a child who rummages in the sand only to find an unexploded mine, she stumbled upon some relatively recent letters inserted between the pages of a deed.

She sat on the floor, her stockings round her ankles. She did not understand much on the first reading. In all of them the signature was just one letter, M, except one which read: "IMA means a thousand prayers for you!" which was impossible to understand. That is, until she found a more recent letter with the ominous M, under which was written in Imre Forgách's handwriting: "Margit sent me this on the sorrowful day that I broke with her," dated according to the Gregorian calendar (well, well).

38

Klara then easily puzzled out the riddle of the other letter: the initials of Imre and Margit were playfully combined to form the word *ima* - prayer. Strangely, the frivolous complicity of that pun hurt Klara more deeply (at least she felt it so at that moment) than a hundred shouted "I love you's" or the most high-flown compliments. She noted that, under the unknown Margit's monogram something was drawn on every letter, a house, an animal, a flower..., and skilfully, it could not be denied.

Instead of a portrait, a silhouette, nothing more. Later Klara inquired about who lived at the Trencsén castle. The owner had been living for a long time in Vienna. For years only German soldiers had been billeted there.

Many people came to the funeral, surprisingly many given Imre Forgách's quiet, withdrawn way of life. Or perhaps the funeral guests honoured him more because of his resigned retreat from life. Maria arranged everything with the greatest decorum. She wept a little too, but after that she stood foolishly, almost absent-mindedly by the coffin, as if she were another one of the dead. She was sad, but her sadness was superficial and isolated; it did not awaken in her the secret depths of bereavement; it did not lead her to the troubled, profound chasms, to those hidden niches where Klara and Susanna (in different ways, naturally) were lamenting the broken roots of their lives and staring into the unclean pit bequeathed to them. Maria's sadness was like a cloak about her shoulders. Though she mourned, she could shut the cellar door behind her and think of the unending cycle of life and death.

Maria was expecting a child.

Only Susanna cried, loudly and convulsively because all the false calm, the forced inner peace of the past year had changed into something wild and desperate, here beside her father's tomb.

16

Peter Bakics arrived at Szklabinya a little before midnight. He had been visiting somewhere in the area, and after he had paid a quick courtesy call on his host (he never stayed anywhere long), he decided to see out the turn of the century with his younger cousins, the Révays.

His thick, black hair gleamed wet; the water trickled down his beard. As he entered the house, melted snow dripped off his fur coat and made thin dark rings on the floor around his boots. He apologised, making excuses for his unexpected arrival; but he laughed as he said it with the self-confidence of one who owns the world, who knows that nobody could be angry with him.

The greyhound immediately fawned on him, planting itself beside him as if they were old companions.

There was nothing very special about Peter Bakics - nothing to excite the poet's pen or troubadour's lyre. Yet there was something mysterious in his eyes, the colour of high hills and dark woods. And perhaps also something in his voice, the running of mountain streams at dawn. Something in his smile, the gentleness of scudding clouds, delightful and natural. Susanna tried to describe him to herself, to deck him out in words, opulently, playfully, to encompass the sort of man he was. But not one of them fit, whatever she tried, this or that, adjectives, super-latives, pejoratives. He could not be summed up.

Peter Bakics embraced and greeted his relations with a cold face and warm hands. "You were just so high when I last saw you," he said, clasping Susanna to him like a child. To Maria he dropped on one knee with more formality, but inclined his head toward her bulging stomach - as if to hear the beating heart of the other newcomer.

They rubbed his wet hair with towels, they dried him, breathed on his neck, fed and watered him. Susanna was surprised when bending down near him with her towel, by the smell of his skin. The fragrance of it was a little like (but different, too) the musician's.

"But this is lovely, I feel like a child again!" laughed Peter Bakics. Susanna held out a clean shirt while the man took off the wet one. She watched as he slid into the other one, as he arranged the sleeves, the collar. She watched, startled and shivering; it seemed as if her sorrow had evaporated. Then she heard her husband's voice asking Peter Bakics whether he had recently been "up there" - it was an expression which often came up in the men's conversation, meaning simply one or other of the Imperial seats, Vienna or Prague. But this is not important now.

Peter Bakics had just finished changing his clothes when the bells rang.

Susanna ran to the windows and opened them.

"We do not want to catch cold," said Maria in a whining voice, she who always sat furthest away from the windows. Susanna obediently pulled the shutters to, making room for Peter Bakics who had stepped into the narrow aperture.

The moon was just a yellow scar, round it were scattered a few tiny, cold, pinprick winter stars. The trees and bushes sat like dark smudges in the valley's hollow. Clean, sharp air flowed into their faces.

Peter Bakics leant out. He loved the pealing bells and the winter fragrance of pines. His dark eyes were alive with tiny roguish lights, radiating warm rays.

Susanna was thinking that something in this man

belonged far more to the valley's deep lap, to the winds
coming off the high hills, to the silence wedged between
the trees and bushes than to the trickling, calculating,
coming-to-nothing conversation going on behind them.

"Just look," said Peter Bakics, "can you see that rock,
a little to the right of the watch-tower light? It's visible
even now, the one pointed like the end of a feather,
that's where the wild sheep live..."

Susanna was astonished. She had never seen it, yet had
looked out of this window hundreds of times.

They turned away only when, after the last chime, they
were greeted with spicy hot wine, with raisins and nuts
(later, plates of food were offered round), and then by
the sound of a painfully beautiful violin. (The musician
was old and decrepit, in his hand the bow trembled,
though it caressed the strings - from whence he came,
where he belonged, who knows?) The seventeenth
century had arrived.

Come one, come all - all aboard for the rickety
merry-go-round of Hungarian history. Just one place left,
this one. It was the first of January, 1600.

They embraced and kissed all around. And Peter
Bakics kissed Susanna Forgách on the mouth. An entirely
casual kiss. And perhaps it was.

Ferenc Révay was overjoyed that he could at last talk
to Maria in peace. She was resting sulkily in the most
comfortable armchair, her arms bent stiffly like carved,
decorated stone (thus the stone lions of Venice hold their
paws). This was primarily because she was angry with her
husband.

Peter Révay had arrived home loaded with presents.
Under his arm he clasped battens of coiled silk in two
shades, one intended for Maria, the other for Susanna.
He had got them cheaply from one of the bankrupt
merchants lounging about in the dark, anarchic halls and
free-market corridors of Hradzsin Castle, waiting, along

with the alchemists, for an audience with the Emperor. (They were certain to achieve this sooner than any foreign delegate or papal nuncio...).

But Maria was not inclined to choose between the silks. If they were not both intended for her, then she did not want either. Since she had become pregnant, she behaved more than ever as if she were both protectress and personification of every lofty moral and cosseted truth. She often turned out her husband's pockets, disbelieving even after the thousandth time that she could find nothing sinful about the poor man, who knew nothing of her suspicions.

So she was pleased that Ferenc Révay had installed himself beside her. Peter Révay just ate and drank, he stuffed himself with food, sweets and meat, as he always did when something happened which he felt was incomprehensible and/or unfair.

Thus Ferenc Révay started to quote by heart (*par coeur* or *fejből*, from the head, as we Hungarians say - whether from head or heart, with ease) from her late father's letter. Maria interrupted - oh, what could be simpler! and with the most skilfully chosen phrases (over-refined people are usually reserved, but at times like this can smear on the muck good and thick) she hissed the story of the music lesson into Ferenc Révay's ear...

How they reached out to each other, how they had touched hands under the musician's cloak, and how Susanna had taken off her ring! That is to say: the virgin and the flute player - she told everything there was to know!

Behold! A lurking suspicion brought to life.

"One more thing, Maria. How far do you think they went?"

Maria smiled (quite exceptionally), the smile of someone who finds a last delicious morsel on what she

believed was an empty plate. She greedily consumed it.
She whispered to Ferenc Révay that she thought *pretty
far...* And then she added poutingly, with a slightly
pathetic seriousness, perhaps the whole way! She immediately promised to make inquiries about the false
musician - to find out where he was living at present. She
could trust someone at Komjáti, if paid well, to gather all
traceable material, fragmentary recollections and gossip
from the period before "our Cyprian" took French
leave...

Ferenc stood up, thanked Maria for everything, and
bade her goodnight. He had (naturally) got a headache
from the over-sweet punch.

He would have liked to talk to Peter Bakics; he was
always glad of his company. The difference between them
was refreshing. While he, Ferenc Révay, dreaded un-
rehearsed conversation, Bakics was surrounded by flitter-
ing, multi-coloured improvisations hatched from personal
experiences, anecdotes and moonshine. No one ever
knew whether even he really believed what he said... Like
a colourful firework spluttering in the air and a very
deep, almost dry well, their opposites attracted each
other...

He looked around.

Susanna was cracking nuts. With obvious pleasure she
picked out the oily pieces from the labyrinths of the
kernel and dropped them one by one into Peter Bakics'
palm.

He looked at his wife in horror. But only at her, he did
not connect the two. The kernels fell to the floor, the
fragments scattered before his eyes, he was devastated,
he was submerged in the past. The disparate elements of
the scene, its dispersed fragments, stayed in his mind...

Glimmers of the future were cast before him, but he
took no notice. He was looking for the stain that Susanna
had wiped on him from the musician's cloak.

17

In the garden the snow began to clear. Black stains from the bonfires celebrating their wedding were again visible.

The unfathomable depths of Ferenc Révay's troubled soul were revealed in the most superficial things. Indeed it was only mundane things which brought the two of them into communication. Would Susanna like a fire at night? He asked her gently, and in this quiet gentleness he looked at his wife as if he were seeing her (a beautiful, exotic creature) for the first time, with a certain open and eager courtesy.

"Yes, that would be very nice," said Susanna, who had shaken with cold all winter. A small, victorious smile spread to the corners of Ferenc Révay's mouth, as if she had betrayed herself as much as he desired. He immediately composed himself (like someone who has just drawn an ace...). Almost playfully he replied (was he hesitating as usual, or simply heightening the enjoyment of putting his new practice into effect?) that it would be wasteful to light fires at night and that cold could not harm God's creatures...

He also developed strange habits.

He pulled out from the depths of one of the mouldering chests a leather-thonged whip, with the smooth, sliding joints of a serpent's body. From then on he always kept it with him, wore it tied round his waist, and wouldn't take it off, not even for a minute. Every now and then he would touch it as if it were a magic charm, a holy amulet.

As Maria's detective work was, for the time being,

ineffectual, Ferenc tried to discover indirectly what he could not find out directly.

In great secret, with threats and the promise of rewards, he had "experts" brought in (too long in the tooth themselves to know anything from experience) to advise what tips and ruses are offered in the ancient book for shamming virginity. Virgo, vagina, vulva - these words rattled in his brain. Why did they all start with the letter V, so like parted legs?

(The idea had been born at the very tomb of his father-in-law, beside the old man's coffin, as Ferenc, his smooth face belying his terrible hatred, regarded the corpse, ostensibly indifferent to the world. Behind Imre Forgách's head the family coat of arms had been placed, supported on a black silk cushion lest it fall over. There a siren figure was seen rising out of the Holy Crown as if from the waves. Thanks to the heraldic maker, the portrayal was exuberantly naturalistic - here was opulent nakedness, bared bosoms, lusty arms, a snail's trail of a navel, all beautifully painted as if alive. The triangle of the mount of Venus adorned the centre of the crown; it was as if the siren held the dead man's head in her lap.)

But the convocation of crones got entangled in debate as they took turns explaining the twenty-two ways of shamming virginity. One swore by soaking an onion in calf's blood, another by dipping a tiny piece of leather in rouge, a third skilfully prepared two sheets. They all praised their own methods, mumbling indignantly against the others'. Finally, in irritation, Ferenc Révay threw them all out, paying them first, of course, to keep their mouths shut. (In those days payment was usually the measure of indiscretion, rather than its opposite.)

Peter Bakics, if he came their way (he was always travelling), was accustomed to look in on Szklabinya. Then Ferenc Révay would quickly comb his hair, straighten his clothes and walk down to the lower gate. Susanna would also come, flustered and blushing. Peter would clasp them both to him. For one he brought news; for the other, small presents.

He took Susanna on his knee - he always called her "my little sister". He inquired about the trivial joys and scandals of the house. How exactly had the lace got torn off her blouse? Why had the roof leaked in the tower room? What could Maria have been thinking of when, in her last letter, she mentioned vague presentiments of bad times ahead? The light talk flitted and circled, but never betrayed what surely must have been the delicious feelings beneath.

Susanna ran to and fro with new liveliness; she bustled about, organising amusements. They would celebrate every possible name day, birthday, wedding and christening, even death was a sweet pretext. Everything became an occasion, let it only be exceptional and rich in ceremony. They might be standing by someone's tomb; the thing that mattered to Susanna was that she was with Peter Bakics. The two measured these moments together, quaking inwardly with overflowing feelings, creating a new centre of the universe.

Peter always arrived full of information. Wherever he went, whether wheeling and dealing in the Imperial halls or in the flea market, he picked up news or slander, it was all the same to him. How different from Ferenc Révay's reticence, his mock-surly manner (and the game of *yes-no* behind which he cultivated his spiritual jungle) which acted as a silencing wall between him and others. By contrast Peter Bakics was a born story-teller, taking enjoyment and delight in fact or fiction.

It was from him that Ferenc Révay first heard about the treason trial which had begun in the Imperial Treasury against one of the country's most respected Protestant lords, a personal friend of the Révay brothers, István Illésházy.

He listened to Bakics' tale with disbelief, stupefied. He was anxious to know whether his brother Peter had already heard about the trial before their last meeting..., somehow this silence on his brother's part worried him more than anything else. He would have preferred to be able to ask the question aloud, with the careful reserve, the revocable, casual ease which was to his taste; but he did not want to mention anything in front of Susanna, absolutely not.

Since her father's death and the appearance of Peter Bakics, Susanna's behaviour had changed towards her husband. She broke her silence, she somewhat forgot her disquiet. A period of misunderstanding and provocation followed between the couple.

(Indeed, when is provocation *not* a matter of mis-understanding? It is the very essence of it: behind the ominous shield, the collective impersonality of the term lurk many implications, and virtually anything is possible: the dripping tap, the invitation to the dance, the Punch and Judy fight.)

In Peter Bakics' company everything culminated. They struggled over nothing and over everything, unendingly. Was the old wine more sour or the new..., was the greyhound really ill or had he just stuffed himself in secret..., would Klara really come and stay, or was she just making another promise...

Susanna had invited, pressed and urged Klara. Ferenc Révay, however, decided that Klara was just right where she was, because (and this argument was truly strange) if she broke her pledge, hey presto! she would fall to pieces. Susanna remonstrated, what was the point of such fidelity to the heavens, when "our dear, sweet father had given her no real cause..." - but her husband just dismissed her, saying, "You naturally would not under-stand such things." On such occasions he would forget the undiminishing hatred he felt towards the dead man. It seemed that Klara's fidelity had transfigured him.

Peter Bakics adapted himself wonderfully to the role of peace-maker, dealing out truth on one side or the other. It seemed as if he could even bring off a victory in the struggle between the couple. As if Peter Bakics could keep them together, by separating and not bridging their differences.

Once Ferenc even said to Peter Bakics, "It's good that you're here; then at least she's in a good mood..."

It seemed he believed it.

Bakics simply raised his head. What response could a man give to these two-faced (perhaps even two-arsed) words? What might they signify? Alms? False gratitude? A confession? A wooden spoon? Luckily, he had nothing to say in reply.

For his part, Ferenc quickly turned away. Because what he had said was not intended as a prelude to disclosing his grievances, as an invitation to be patronised or as a first concealed, poisoned barb, not at all. It had simply popped out of him without his thinking, a tiny, graceful bubble of relief.

From now on he would strive to maintain the facade intact, to foster illusion and keep it separate from reality, once and for all.

Whereas "up there" - at mad Rudolf's - the windows were pitch black, the palace seemed uninhabited, but inside, the Emperor's innermost chamber was warmed by dozens of candles and bathed in the light of torches, here at Szklabinya it was just the opposite. Ferenc Révay was happy that at last there was something to brighten the facade, to keep the exterior welcoming, to hide all the better, while it could, the desolation within. Now time was of the essence for him; or at least that is what he kept saying to himself. Like hammer blows, so often did this word *time* appear in the anguished and cock-eyed plans in his diary, at his wilful core, in that childish heart where he had decided that his soul could struggle and whimper as much as it liked, but that he must keep Susanna Forgách at all costs. He felt this was his right, a notion fed on vague notions of destiny and a wild desire to possess. This triumphed over his feelings of guilt, lessening his intimations of shame, although of course the shame did not disappear completely. He became in this strange, double-edged, smothering state, like a baby being lulled to sleep.

The Cradle of Guilt
(A History Lesson in a Slip of the Pen)

Lapsus calami, Lapsus calami! crowed all the cocks in the councillors' ears, from the moment they took part in the treason trial of István Illésházy.

This trial - "the mirror of the age", as our textbooks might put it - was not a show trial in the contemporary and well-remembered sense of the word: the accused did not have to accept responsibility for imaginary and trumped-up "crimes", not at all. The subject of the trial - a pretext with a glimmer of truth in it - is not worth bothering about, really. (Age-old patterns feed off whatever history offers - titbits, souvenirs, tourist menus. It just depends on your point of view...) Perhaps it was simply that Emperor Rudolf, with some half-justified, half-devious motives, promised to grant a Royal Charter to two of István Illésházy's towns. Illésházy protested once and then again... The classic conflict of central power and feudal privilege that we learnt about at school, nothing more.

The personal dimension of this public event is perhaps due - in a part of the world like ours - to the appearance in our history of an absolutist will (History's pointed arrow?) in the mind of an alien tyrant... Is it not possible that all this historical blood and sweat (whose blood, and whose sweat?) spilt elsewhere - on the territories of a more independent state - might be overcome without leaving a lasting impression? Whereas here all survival and power, all construction and effort of will (as ever, political interference comes from the higher ranks, not the others, poor things...) depends in the final analysis on the suspended sword and false promises of an alien power... This can sow only guilt in the national consciousness. (Certainly, ethological comparisons between the histories of subordinate and independent nations would be well worth a mass...)

To resume, this trial was a cradle of guilt. It filled the participants with shame, as is evident in the astonishing fact that neither the accused nor the judge could remember anything about it afterwards - although it severely tried a generation's faith (and both of them were excellent historians, too!). Not even when they could have done so in peace (or, shall we say, with tranquil hearts).

The accused remained silent about his years of torment and persecution; and the judge, Istvánffy, only mentioned a few words about the case. His clutching at self-justificatory straws revealed both the accused's innocence and his own (non-partisan) interest, as in his insistence that the verdict was not unanimous, but the work of a mere majority.

I should say that the twenty members of the Judicial Council were without exception Hungarian. This included György Thurzó.

György Thurzó, a privy councillor, was the Forgách girls' step-cousin on their mother's side, and was also a close relation and fairly good friend of the Révays. Peter Révay, chiefly in letters, always used the epithet "our friend" for Thurzó, which was understandable, as he really was a family friend although still a grand relation, in whose warm, radiating light one could bathe.

György Thurzó was trusted by the group of courtiers who gathered round Archduke Mátyás, their organiser-in-chief. Peter Révay, by contrast, wandered left (and right), like a lost lamb in this circle: if he was present, he clutched his coat of arms like a Royal Pardon. He was like a cat on hot bricks, especially if he felt the approaching whirlwind of intrigue and scandal. In such things he looked up to György Thurzó as simply as a child would do.

Archduke Mátyás, the Emperor's brother, who had been expelled from Prague without word or document, by sheer force of arms, was at this moment preparing in Vienna (quietly tying up the threads), a very carefully thought-out war against Rudolf's rule. Hence he now revealed that he was a supporter of the Hungarians and Protestants (it was not, and would not, always be so...).

Who is not familiar with the swings and round-abouts of political alliances and other such tactical ephemera, with all their primitive logic? Must one say it was a fiasco?

György Thurzó was a honey-tongued, devilish-looking man. With his pinned-back ears, his shaggy black hair, he reminded one of drawings of that amiable, fleeing devil well known to iconography.

"My God, how different from Peter Bakics' black locks" (Susanna Forgách).

His hands were also covered with curly hair: this was most apparent when he explained or argued about something, because he would rub his hands together incessantly (quite common among such types).

Spirited and faithful Protestant (discreetly). Spirited and faithful monarchist (openly). That is to say all the contradictions of the period (hawking and cawing) were embedded in his fissured soul (his too). He was proud that the two inmates in his soul got on together in peace, without stirring up trouble.

He felt the honour and importance of his dual mission keenly, was both devoted bearer and weary trustee. Although inwardly his vainglory and pride swelled, outwardly he lamented his role to the world (a fashionable gesture of the romance of Hungarian history).

In any event György Thurzó was trying with considerable skill to bridge the gap between the Hapsburg Archduke and his own hard-pressed compatriots.

Maria also thought highly of him (she was never one to spurn the aura of rank and power). She was always inviting him to stay, to celebrations, sending presents to his wife. But he did not accept these invitations from his "loving cousins" as frequently as Maria would have liked and hoped. She called him "my brother". In her diary she wrote, "if my brother were here". This took on the same sort of fanciful and imperative meaning as "Trencsén business" had had in Klara's imagination.

However, Ferenc Révay was annoyed by the family worship of Thurzó. He did not really believe in Thurzó's political hopes, in his labyrinthine alliances, in his sham religious freedom, or in the rising star at court of his Reformist relatives and friends (indeed, soon to be a falling star).

But he kept his doubts to himself because he did not trust anyone, not even his own brother.

How long can a person be both a staunch Protestant and a staunch Hapsburg monarchist? One is a cup of coffee, the other a glass of milk. All one can do is stir them together and sugar well. Ferenc could not understand it. He felt that he was completely lost and entangled in this devil's web, woven from frog's spit, spider's silk, and toad's slime (and of course history). The public mind had cut a formless mass into four camps: pro-Monarchist, pro-Turk, Catholic, Protestant. He did not know what to do with four camps, let alone when they were further sub-divided by religion into opposing strands. Of the four camps only one was deserted: the Catholic-Turkish. In the other three, relatives, friends and acquaintances were dispersed on all sides. There were those who stood with both feet planted firmly in a single camp, on chosen and/or designated ground. There were others with one foot in one camp and the other in another, throwing out their chests like Gargantua (now in yet a third role...?). While others half-heartedly or deviously gave only provisional support to a single side. They looked to whichever of the converging axes had a stronger point of alignment, so they could shift the sooner.

Ferenc was inclined to distance himself as far as possible from the court.

But from a distance he still followed events with lively interest, even with intimate knowledge - his usual show of indifference naturally concealed this well.

Susanna did not particularly like Thurzó. She did not really see him as a brother, either. She found him a little repugnant; she was even a little afraid of him, as she was of everyone who treated lightly those things that did not immediately relate to the weighty and secretive matters on which religions or nations stood or fell...

For Thurzó everything that happened outside this sphere was dust and ashes. The only white swan in his soul was his love for his wife. This tender relationship he set on a high pedestal; it was his one relaxation and secret refuge. His yearning letters to his precious and honoured Elizabeth comprised several volumes. It was as if he crammed everything which he would not acknowledge in others into this singular relationship. But it was not simply a matter of special esteem or superficial grace. He, who elsewhere wore a severe public mask, revealed in the letters he wrote to Elizabeth Czobor his unashamed frivolity: "You are the nicest bed warmer, my sweet heart! Your loving companion, who loves you as himself." Could there be a more perfect combination of tenderness and raw soul than this valediction? (Perhaps the siege of Esztergom and the intrigues of the Viennese Court were not the only ways to self-knowledge...)

Wherever György Thurzó went the most important thing - could it be more important than affairs of state? - was that he should provide his love Elizabeth with the fruits of the season, if not in abundance, then at least with some frequency. He always counted them assiduously; thirty-two oranges and three pomegranates, or perhaps only twelve oranges, but five honey melons as well... Thus oranges would reach Elizabeth even during the biggest blood bath - love oranges, blood oranges (the easiest way to obtain them on siege territory was via the enemy supply-lines).

But György Thurzó did not willingly write about the stormy affairs of the *vita publica* to his wife. Although his loving Elizabeth was grateful for the fruit, she appealed for news from the front, information, scraps, all in vain.

But this time György Thurzó was reluctant to set forth. On the night before his journey he locked all his private papers and letters in a trunk. He dipped into it, reading a bit here and there. Elizabeth urged him. "You must get up early," she said. She was less anxious about his getting up at dawn than about his interest in concealing those papers.

"You can never tell," Thurzó replied, for once not as a tactic nor from any false sense of delicacy (although they were indispensable to him normally...). He himself did not know exactly, and would have had difficulty explaining precisely the sort of lurking, whispering feelings behind the seventh closed door of his soul, which sensed danger and told him to stow his letters and papers under the bed.

To prepare for all eventualities, Elizabeth chose woollen stockings, the green ones which he rarely wore because he did not like the colour. In them he hid the keys to the chest, among the underwear, deep down. "Let's hope this is unnecessary," said Elizabeth Czobor while she placed the shirts, underskirts and towels above, all starched and bleached and beautifully folded.

Thurzó looked at the rounded hips that he had to leave behind, laying his hands on them. At dawn he dressed, grumbling, cursing the bloody rain, the pools of mud. He clambered awkwardly into the coach and bemoaned his fate. "I will try to send fruit," he whispered in farewell.

During the journey he had time to think, plenty of it. Before him lay the grey, misty, tail-between-its-legs, ear-flattened winter landscape. For once he really did not know what to do. His heart was overflowing with self-pity. And once a man gets into this state, however much his soul struggles and writhes, nothing can be done. It can only get worse.

"This miserable land over which I travel is spread out before me..." (complaining letter to Elizabeth Czobor).

On the day of his arrival he carefully read through the charge. Between the lines, behind the authoritative manner and spidery writing, it spewed out...

The charge was made on twelve counts. It included everything. Even what the accused had said once, years before, to a bath attendant. While stretched out pleasantly, skin tingling at the touch of starched linen and the heat of the sauna, his pores opening as he fell into an easy, communicative state, then (reportedly) István Illésházy had remarked with relaxed and patronising carelessness, in front of said attendant (the point being not what he said, but in front of whom he said it), that these Germans were truly awful. But this was no worse than any exploited and intimidated peasant, burgher or noble might have said openly in the streets...

Perhaps the best would be to protest, to stage a boycott, to prove with actions instead of words that the charges were feeble and fabricated from thin air?

Or perhaps precisely because of this, it was not worth taking too seriously, a protest might dignify the half-blown affair and these shop-window proceedings. (A lofty viewpoint, but not easy to adopt, for the more groundless the charge, the more dangerous it is!)

Thurzó took comfort that the defendant was such a favoured, generally esteemed and high-ranking personage. Nothing worse could happen to him than once in a blue moon happened to the minor, less-respected aristocracy.

The embarrassed, hesitant members of the Judicial Council sought each other out. They made enquiries before the first hearing in twos, or at most threes. They talked unceasingly. And yet in such exploratory situations, especially within such a conciliatory group (it is exactly this which is so fascinating, is it not?) it is easier to come to a (seemingly) unanimous decision (without too much trouble) when there is one over-riding interest...

The key to the situation was mad Rudolf's offended pride. Therefore it would not be prudent to make a scandal of it and blow it up further. This would be sheer irresponsibility! Better to try to sweeten Rudolf's incensed, self-important proceedings with the colourless (and hypocritical) nosegay of unanimity, with make-believe gestures to forgo parliamentary jurisdiction, so that they could deal with the matter privately and in peace. Then the Emperor could have a private audience with the defendant, who would, face-to-face and kneeling, give his *mea culpa* and ask respectfully for pardon. ("A short, sharp lecture would not hurt Illésházy, he's been conceited enough recently...").

It was in this spirit that the Judicial Council assembled the following day - without all members present, however.

Some of them merely sent their decisions in writing in advance; paying lip-service to the pre-requisites of justice. They soothed their troubled consciences by writing that they *strictly conditionally* (!) accepted that Illésházy was guilty if he had committed all that the threadbare charge enumerated against him. *If...* This was the hole in the fence that the fox would slip through - all shame and doubt were whitewashed by this word.

Thus five of them excused themselves, referring to their troubles, their illnesses, even gout (behold, the age of the jolly toper's malady). Only one of them - who knew the procedures - can be properly called defiant. His strict standard of decency could not be impugned, either then or later. His name was Ferenc Nádasdy, who was, incidentally, husband to the bloodthirsty Elizabeth Báthory. To digress just a little more: his son Paul Nádasdy was soon to be husband to Judith Révay, who had waited with a beating heart, hearkening for Peter Bakics on that same clear night of the new century on which he leant his tousled head toward Maria Forgách's swelling belly...

During the Judicial Council's hearing, the representatives of the Imperial Treasury painted the charges in the expected spiteful and malicious colours. One of them, the cock-sure Janos Joó, had long harboured a personal dislike and desire for revenge against the accused. (We will later see the result of his disloyalty.) The other Imperial representative, István Szuhay, Bishop of Eger, was the son of a butcher, who had struggled diligently in the post of Treasurer, and who was also full of welling hatred for the wealthy aristocrat.

This type will appear for a long time yet on the donkey-eared pages of the romance of Hungarian history. We will meet with it under other names (Romance II): there will be György Szelepcsényi, Archbishop of Kalocsa, not Bishop of Eger, that's true, and he will call his Emperor Leopold, not Rudolf. Another one of sober and devout nature (but that does not change the seriousness of the sentences the defendants received). Those defendants, however, have not been born yet... Although little Judith (the one whose heart throbbed, etc.) will give birth to a son called Ferenc after his grandfather, Judith Révay will not live to see Szuhay's descendants clap and whoop at her son's death sentence...because more than fifty years must pass before the continuation of this Judas death dance. The treacherous dance of death, again and again and again.

The same scenario with different props, transformed and reincarnated patterns and types.

Just now they are giving out the tickets to this sorrowful ride through the centuries.

György Thurzó was so astonished at the harsh tone of the Treasurer, at the ice-cold seriousness of his face, that his mouth pouted pathetically as he analysed and weighed up the charges.

But he joined in loudly, nodding approvingly. The summing-up flashed by, so that there was no turning back or chance for hesitation. *What was done...was done.* In this sighing, broken way Thurzó tried, at first to himself and then to others, to justify his conduct. (His whole conception of the world might also be summed up by this long-standing tautology.) However, the sad, suspended pronoun *what* cannot readily be replaced with, let us say, the word "honour"... Perhaps he himself, with natural modesty, would have been surprised if someone had tried to read into his little euphemism a statement of principle.

"The crime that Illésházy committed against the King was not trifling. Therefore punishment is unavoidable..." so declared the Judicial Council. And the decision was handed over to the Treasury officials...and taken triumphantly, with as much flag-waving as they pleased, straight to Prague. In order - and this is important - to avoid Hungarian parliamentary jurisdiction.

And what of the accused?

He was downcast, dumb-founded, but inwardly calm.

He wrote another letter to Rudolf, tried to break through the wall of silence.

Even if only with half a shoulder.

One thing annoyed him, indeed, bothered him

exceedingly: Thurzó's behaviour.

He had expected better of him.

But then he dismissed it. In friendly company (for how long? This would still remain to be seen...) he cheerfully announced that he was not a bit shaken, he always knew the noble György Thurzó was the biggest turncoat around, isn't that so?

His friends just hummed and nodded their heads, smiling: "*That's the way life is...* But at least spring has finally arrived. And after all, we're not all like that..."

62

18

"Turncoat."

They said it many times one after another, *turncoat.*
And laughed a lot.

Ferenc Révay hummed, unable to conceal his delight,
when Peter Bakics told him (he had heard it in Pozsony)
what Illésházy had said about Thurzó to the large
company assembled in Vienna's *Weeping Willow* tavern.

Ferenc savoured the word. But he did not want to
disclose his feelings towards Thurzó in front of Bakics,
who was a devout Catholic. Indeed, he had been a papal
knight.

A papal knight - Susanna often repeated this to
herself. The papal honour had become the stuff of her
day-dreams, their focus and song, without her really
knowing what it meant. But she felt it must be something
important, at the very least connected with the suffering,
all-secret, all-sighing, all-woeful haloes of the Chosen
Ones.

At night she dreamt about it too. In her dream she was
playing in the Pope's halls. His Holiness got off his
throne when she entered. He hurried towards her,
embraced her, his huge rings imprinting her uncovered
shoulders; she made excuses for her decolletage, as only
on the threshold of the bedchamber had she realised that
she was not wearing the most suitable clothes for this
occasion, but by then it was too late. But the Pope just
waved his hand and pressed her to him even more
closely. He led her to the innermost compartment in a
secret cupboard, and as they went he explained that this

way they would be safe from the prying eyes of the cardinals behind them. From the cupboard he retrieved the Virgin Mary's veil, the arrows of Saint Sebastian, one by one, with roses of coagulated brown-red blood at their tips, then Saint Cecilia's snow-white violin, and Susanna gently ran her fingers over the strings. He dusted off Moses' stone tablets before handing them to her, saying that this was all just provincial museum stuff. She dared not ask what she most wanted to, but His Holiness was wonderfully perceptive. He smiled at Susanna, digging his rings deeper into her flesh, which hurt. But she smiled back and then at last the Pope came to the most important thing: he gave a brief account, rich in praises of Lord Bakics' distinctions...to him alone are we indebted that these many sacraments, this sainted shrine itself is still intact! While the squeaking chorus of cardinals could be heard fervently applauding in the background, His Holiness softly, and perhaps a little familiarly, asked whether Susanna Forgách knew why he, the Pope, was telling all this to her alone?

Susanna was going to ask precisely the same question (but then she woke up).

At about this time (later several others would refer to it from the witness box) she began to ask those around her, hesitating at first, but afterwards more boldly ("then I knew that something was not quite right between the married couple"), if it was possible, whether it was possible (if, if...), "Is true love possible without lust?"

But most of those questioned just shrugged their shoulders... *That* certainly was not love... The priest declared love is something in which (God sees, Satan laughs) there always lurks a core of lust, the mischievous sprite of sensuality.

And Peter Bakics? He sent a message that he would look in at Szklabinya on his way to a local cattle market. And at the appointed hour he arrived.

Thus on an early summer's eve when warm winds rustled, whipping in the air the broken wings and tatters of white flowers, and the waters flowed in the stream beds, Susanna was waiting, radiant, to receive Peter Bakics.

She had placed candles in all the windows and lattices of the castle. By the time they were all lit, on the ground floor, on the top floors, in the crevices of the tower (it was not easy, when one of them finally flamed, another somewhere was going out with a tiny fizzle, so that she had to hurry up and down from one floor to the other) dusk was falling. Susanna shepherded everyone into the garden to see from which point the spectacle would look most beautiful. Earlier the reddening light of the setting sun had almost eclipsed the candles in their modest, doleful sanctuary lamps. Now in the grey dusk they burned orange, they were bright flames of true love, eternal fires of blind suffering, a victorious procession. Now not only did they array the castle, its ledges and sills, but they created it in their own image against an enveloping darkness.

And while the others were all streaming out into the open air, Susanna Forgách clasped Peter Bakics by the hand and, helter-skelter, pulled him into her room, embraced him, kissed him, and whispered into his soft beard that she waited only for him, thought of him every day, because he was the only ray of light in her wretched life, her winter moon, her guiding star, her scripture and her sacred book, her silence and her song, her life-line, her lucky charm, her mirror and the centre of her life, in short, that she desired Peter Bakics. She really did have all these dim feelings, but afterwards even she did not know how much she had revealed in that shadowy corner of her darkening room. It was certainly quite enough; for Peter Bakics replied in his deep, melodious voice, "Don't talk such nonsense!"

But after all, he did suffer Susanna to kiss him; and he did, naturally, respond. The kiss lasted only as long as is proper for a first kiss, that is, a good while... After the first, uncertain parting of their lips, Peter Bakics kissed Susanna quickly on the forehead (as if he could abate reeling desire and coursing blood with a brotherly gesture, the seal of a brother's love...).

He held Susanna's face between his palms and explained to her that her beauty had indeed stricken his heart then and there, the moment the New Year bells had rung, but until now this beauty had been a closed book to him ("because you know, Susaka, I am not a trouble-making type..."). Then he kissed her again.

Meanwhile Ferenc Révay was looking for his wife in the garden, among the slate-blue bushes (in vain, we know).

Now everything became nothing to Susanna Forgách. The mystery of life and spiritual despair, the great questions and crosses to bear were as nothing. Her husband's strange changes of mood, the anxiety about whether she could prise open the fragile lock of his reserve, all became nothing. Indeed she was almost, nay, entirely happy that her marriage was careful diplomacy and nothing else. Both future and past were now as nothing - one was empty and cold like an unused cellar; the other, more ephemeral than a rainbow. She thought only of the present, that moment which billowed and rolled. The rest just dwindled away. Her *sweet nothing* state flowed from this: *sweet* was all the hopeful wait and raging joy when Peter Bakics would finally arrive and clasp her to him, his beard brushing her neck or face for just a moment. And *nothing* was everything else. That is, nearly everything else.

Need we say more about the feverish symptoms of awakened love (or the *suspicion-arousing syndrome*)?

During that summer Peter Bakics was almost always

either at the Révays' - playing cards, discoursing, making merry, attending celebration after celebration - or on the way to see them. (And Susanna, from the moment they bade farewell, spent every minute awaiting his return.)

Once when they went out by wagon down into the valley, Peter Bakics embraced Susanna in his usual way; and his hand...his hand wandered freely beneath her light summer blouse. Yet it stopped, stopped dead on the curve of her ribs, going neither higher nor lower.

On another occasion Ferenc had to go away for a few days. Then Susanna wove her hands around Peter Bakics' neck - the dust of the departure was still whirling by the castle gate. Her palms softly supported his nape - or rather with woven fingers she gently took the scruff of the man's neck, saying, "At last we can be together for a whole night."

But Peter Bakics only kissed first her nose, then her face, then her mouth with light kisses.

"We must go no further, it's forbidden. Everything will be spoilt."

This was his reply.

19

The nights were growing colder; longer and longer the hills were swathed in darkness.

Only Ferenc Révay was not enlightened (although the whispering and muttering in the castle was at its height...).

He knew nothing. That summer, if anything, Susanna had been a little kinder towards him. The considerate gesture, the welcoming smile...clearly a few morsels had inevitably fallen from her secret cargo of desire. Ferenc Révay even thought of becoming closer to his wife.

Maria Forgách's letter also had an effect on him. She had at last tracked down *that wretched musician*, "... my brother helped me." Ferenc hoped Thurzó had not become involved in the affair, but he was greatly interested in the information.

According to Maria - incredibly! - the fake musician was living at the Emperor's court and ("hold tight, my dear, sweet Ferenc!") he was according to some, Master Basirius, leader of the alchemist circle in Prague with direct access to the Emperor, to whom he made daily reports. Others said he had assumed the name of Beltegeuze Antares Rigel and practised astrology, dancing attendance on the great Kepler and, once again, completely at home in the Imperial Palace.

Everyone knew the Palace was like a gypsy camp, where showmen, quack doctors with pockets bulging, camped in the corridors, and card-sharpers slid down the banisters. Or perhaps a marketplace offers a more apt description: closets in all the ante-rooms were full to bursting with test tubes, bubbling brews, glass balls, hocus-pocus, kaleidoscopes and metre-long telescopes. Steam from wild concoctions floated freely through the rooms; dead cats and exhumed skeletons were dragged along the finely decorated corridors. Recently one had even scratched the wonderful marble inlay, *rat-a-tat-tat...*

The grip of Ferenc's old jealousy loosened a little, and he stopped prowling around the castle.

The truth was that Ferenc Révay became more and more hopeful of clearing everything up, of "taking the necessary steps" (this is how he summed it up). He strung his tangled hopes on a weak thread - naturally forgetting the original sequence of things.

Thus one evening he came to knock on his wife's door with feelings of relief. He sat down without speaking, and then began. He began, and this is important, because in their fragile relationship, their glass marriage, he had often thought about who would speak first and whether to employ subterfuge or to pretend innocence..., in short, he began to speak, at first saying only how beautiful the coverlet was, how it seemed, sadly enough, that autumn had arrived early, then mentioning, "I want to talk to you..."

But Susanna just sat in front of the mirror brushing her hair, making a great play of it, without even turning round. She replied that Klara had sent the coverlet, and, yes, she hated the wind.

How to go on? Perhaps like this? "We must talk"- but he did not think that was suitable. He whined inwardly, he felt the words crumbling, hollow words. He always found the inner silence of words to be painful and dangerous, and now the indolent indifference of nature also offended him - the leaves streaming from the branches outside the window became a shower of exclamation marks.

Normally he would have gone away.

But he went on; he had gone past the point of no return: "I know that I am at fault."

He saw that his wife, who had been pinning up her hair, had dropped the hair pins in some confusion. Then with a practised movement she hung some sort of oblong stone in her ear (how it stayed there, suspended, was impossible to tell). She returned to her hair (now no longer completely loose). She did not pin it up further, she simply held it up, and in the mirror he saw her take out the drops from her ears once again.

He did not understand the whole operation, the torment; but of course he had never understood such things. For his part, he was surprised, he almost shuddered at the hitherto unknown, rapturous and self-revelatory feelings which flooded and welled up inside him. How easy everything was! He must simply allow these revealing, breaking waves, this cascade, to flow forth; perhaps it would be easier still... This is what he was feeling as Susanna finally turned towards him and smiled.

"Give me your hand," she said.

He went towards her and - for once without hesitation - obeyed.

Susanna took his hand and held it, as if she were seeing it for the first time. Then she let go and placed it next to hers, so that their hands floated in the air like resting birds. At last she said jauntily, with an air of expectant pleasure - like someone who looks out of the window and says, "Hoorah, the sun is shining!"- that both their wrists were thinner than Peter Bakics'.

Then, more with quiet dismay than anything else, Ferenc asked her (or rather stated, because these things cannot really be asked, but must simply be refined with interrogative emphasis), "Are you ill?"

Susanna Forgách (her hair on her shoulders, the ear-drops on the table) stood up and looked straight into her husband's face with dreamy, leaf-green eyes.

"*You* are asking me?"

Afterwards Ferenc Révay was not able to say exactly what it was that turned him inside out like a threadbare coat. His wounded pride? His profane desires? His repeated failure as a man?

He struck at Susanna's face, and struck again and again, whether with the whip or not, he was unsure. Susanna got hold of it, but he snatched it out of her hands. Later, witnesses would disagree about this. (How did they draw conclusions? Did they peep through the key hole? It was not locked, or probably not...)

In any case they all agreed that the Mistress got hold of the whip at last and cut it into pieces with some implement lying at hand. Then the Master had grabbed a book, one with a clasp and decorative cover, possibly some kind of poetry or prayer book, and smote the Mistress with it, whose delicate skin was immediately broken... One of the servants, who on hearing the screaming and shrieking had rushed to the scene, testified she had seen with her own eyes the Mistress sitting, feeling the fresh wounds on her face, her eyes glassy as if she had just seen a ghost or a miracle, and the Master fallen on his knees before her, imploring her that everything would be all right...

But they, the witnesses that is, could not guess what this "everything" was!

However it happened, one thing is certain; not a single element was missing from this familiar drama of passion and remorse.

At least for one party.

Because for the other - for Susanna - there remained only a great and obdurate resolve. She could not even cry.

Her husband hid his head in the clouds - the weather had recently taken on a mythological significance in Susanna's life. Especially in the autumn-winter months, she felt that everything depended on it, namely whether Peter Bakics would set out, or arrive. Fog at dawn, drizzle (not to speak of snowfalls) filled her with real terror. Would the horses stumble? Would his carriage get stuck?

20

But Peter Bakics did arrive.
Ferenc did not bear the slightest grudge towards him.

He did not connect the two events, regarding Susanna's behaviour as merely a smoke-screen, a childish game, a mannerism.

The tumultuous and chaotic emotions flowing between them all were like birds trying to fly in a dense wood.

Especially as Peter Bakics was Ferenc's only really good friend. That is to say, the arrival of Peter Bakics was the only thing that brightened Révay's difficult life. Sometimes he would jealously try to keep the visitor to himself, to talk to him privately; but then Susanna would play possessive and wreck everything.

Ferenc invited the visitor to ride with him on his dawn rounds; out on the rambling, soft hills they could talk.

"I hear not all is well between you two..." (Peter Bakics, extremely cautiously).

"Has she been complaining?"

"She just mentioned something."

Ferenc accepted this reproof without a word. He was almost pleased, because at that time his soul was still remorseful. They went down towards the stables.

Bakics acted as if he had no notion of his own leading role in the events, even though Susanna had told him everything blow by blow. Later (when their love was at that tender, myth-creating stage), Peter Bakics would tell Susanna, "It was probably then that I fell in love with you!" He embroidered this by recalling the new, hitherto unknown feelings awakened in him when she had examined his wrist. Then passion and ecstasy had taken root, and he felt as if he had been anointed with a great burning mission to open the closed door of Fate and unmask evil and deceit!

The two men trotted briskly along together over the mud-spattered grass, on the rain-drenched fields the sky's grey cut off the corners of the horizon, rounding them off - as if angels had wreathed muslin about their heads, about this piece of earth.

Peter said it must never happen again.

Ferenc Révay replied that Peter could be sure of it. He, Ferenc, could not imagine life without Susanna Forgách.

This rang surprisingly true. Although perhaps the silence and emptiness of the landscape added a ring of truth to his statement (just the two of them, and the two horses), peeling off the social polish and grime, the "I can retract" cover from the words, lifting them from their bed of relativity, or rather flicking them into a different, more resonant chamber where every word articulated was like embarking on a spiritual exercise... Perhaps this revelatory mood can explain why Ferenc, who had never initiated anything in his life, started to speak to Peter Bakics about his wife and the musician.

Saying that even now he was not sure what had actually happened between them.

Bakics just smiled. He would not have been disturbed even if everything had happened. His attitude to past affairs of the heart was *what is done is done*. Later, when Susanna spoke to him about Cyprian Virgil Basirius, insisting it had all been just a childish game, innocent fun, Peter just laughed and said, "You love me - you only *liked* him. So he can only be jealous of me!"

And he really believed it.

But perhaps it was his too-easy smile, his expectant silence, his naive and intent look that gave Ferenc Révay, on this misty dawn ride, the thought that perhaps Peter Bakics was the go-between for Susanna and the musician...

("He travels enough.")

Ferenc thought it all out later, after Bakics had left.

"One-eyed," he finally said. It seemed, in that web of emotion in which virtue and its opposite struggled with equal force, just at that moment he had uncovered the musician's final mask.

But Bakics interjected that he would like to turn to more serious things.

Ferenc was starved for news, "Have you heard anything?"

Bakics said that more trials would probably follow... But when Ferenc asked who would be next, he replied, "I do not know," with such resigned simplicity, with such a heavy downward look, it was as if he held in his hands all the questions and possible answers, as if questions, answers and all attendant deliberations pointed at Ferenc Révay.

However, Bakics promised he would enquire further in Vienna before the end of the winter.

When he bade farewell to Susanna (as if he knew that this would be the last occasion of the year), he kissed her without any brotherly or my-little-sisterly hocuspocus (whispering, "Your mouth tastes like an almond!").

"If there is any trouble write or send word, and you know I will come," adding for emphasis - "immediately."

Wild winds blew down from the hills; the first snow fell. It lay on the peaks and enveloped the roads in ice. It was almost impossible to leave the castle.

Peter Bakics did not return during these winter months. The other two remained shut up, snowed in.

Face to Face
(History Lesson No.2)

There was silence from the Imperial Treasury at
Prague after the Judicial Council rendered its first
decision. A ponderous silence.

Rudolf did not reply to the accused's letter. Nor
did he give any signal to the councillors. It seemed
that nothing would open the iron-barred, purgatorial
gates to his vortical, occult-obsessed mind. He held
fast at the threshold, where trusted servants and
ornamental Cerberuses guarded the entrance.

Archduke Mátyás approved of the Council's
solution to the affair. Thurzó's clever tactics suited
his own designs: to nod, yes, whosoever is guilty, is
guilty..., to bend the knee before the Emperor, and
thus slip the conclusion of the trial skilfully past the
difficult and public parliamentary forum into a light,
traceless private occasion.

("Whosoever is guilty, is guilty" - behold yet
another tautology! Moral and spiritual trials are
avoided beautifully with this linguistic device in the
"petit-bourgeois" university of life, according to the
clever Roland Barthes. We might also humbly add
that this applies as well to the moral-miasmatic and
device-ridden university of politics.)

György Thurzó stayed in Vienna. He managed to
obtain for his wife two oranges and three lemons, a
little unripe, but no matter. He sent sticky concoctions from the palace doctors and opaque drops
from the market. Sometimes he sent a dozen letters
home at once. He carefully reported on his state of

health, chiefly his daily rhythm of digestion. He also calculated Elizabeth's cycle ("I trust you are postponing it, my sweetheart, that we may be blessed with grandchildren to hold in our arms, my love.").

As usual he said little about his troubled spirit. Elizabeth probably knew nothing about all that had happened during the first sitting of the Judicial Council, although Thurzó thought of nothing else (his digestive problems were certainly all due to his tension and brooding). In this trap of his own making, he weighed up pros and cons, means and ends continuously. Supposing he had miscalculated when he had loudly chimed in with Szuhay? If perchance the game was not simply to wrap the mottled bean of vanity in a small bag and shake it a little (but rather fortunes, possessions, goods and chattels)?

He could not bear the waiting. He *must* take steps before it was too late - take the initiative, knock on doors, speak out, persuade the Archduke to break the ominous silence.

The Judicial Council was summoned once more to vote: private audience or public jurisdiction? - in other words, to couch in official written form that which, up until now, they had tried (without result) to pass to the Emperor through the highest and most intimate channels.

Archduke Mátyás's behaviour was cold and correct. He merely registered his personal wishes in one cautious and artful half-sentence (no need to finish it, everybody knew what it was): "The offence to His Majesty is in this case so great that it is only possible (read "enough" in place of "only possible") to atone for it face to face..."

From his lips - one imagines - half a sentence was more than enough for most of them...

Not quite.

Four councillors stood out against it openly as a group. (Including Ferenc Nádasdy who, although he only wrote a letter, used the strongest possible words.)

Three voted for the extraordinary hearing, albeit in a roundabout way, with dialectical intricacy. (Among them Bishop Ferenc Forgách.)

Four demanded a public sentence for the accused (the Treasury spokesman Szuhay and the personally affronted Joó were naturally among them).

The others foraged under the table, not showing their hands for either "yes" or "no".

The Archduke sent an accompanying letter with the majority verdict, in which he pressed certain arguments on Rudolf. For example: Illésházy was so well loved that if he were given a severe sentence, "there could be certain diverse changes of mood." (The most pressing reasons for this political champing-at-the-bit and squabbling were not alluded to.) The question was, why did the Archduke write "diverse" and not the more expressive word "dangerous"? However, given mad Rudolf's nature, we should not be at all surprised at this sly omission.

But the Illésházy affair had become emblematic of the Hapsburgs' internecine war. Thus the more the Archduke sought to protect the accused, the more Rudolf gave a free hand to his greedy Treasury (for the present).

First this and then that...blind hope and tireless diligence (a good many entries could be added to our "political dictionary"...).

Rudolf nodded roguishly at his younger brother's lengthy letter. Oh yes! yes! An extraordinary audience, that would really be the best; in that way one could get nicely acquainted with this great and famous lord, the accused, and then we can have a pleasant conversation about this and that, painting and astronomy perhaps, why not?

But Szuhay was getting impatient. He muttered and hissed in Rudolf's ear that it was absolutely necessary to issue a decree. A hint of private intrigue, that symbol of weakness, and people would whisper and snigger. The ruler drank in his hatred: who knows what might be brewing against the Emperor's royal person? Thus Szuhay convinced the Emperor behind closed doors. Though we should say bars rather than doors - Rudolf had placed bars around his bed, and had also divided off the dining table with iron stakes. Even with the keys in his pocket, he was frightened. He would wake in the night filled with fear. With trembling hands, with clinking and clashing, he would open the iron gate around his bed and then his chamber door. He would search the castle, along the guarded corridors, roaming the whispering galleries, running for his life, howling, from the pounding force of evil.

No one could sleep because of this nerve-wracking death yell, ever a false alarm.

Szuhay sought and found new arguments. Drawing on the treasure chest of history, like cards from his sleeve, he maintained that an offence as grave as Illésházy's was last committed a century earlier, when Ulászló Lorinc Ujlaky had been publicly denounced as an idiot!

(Poor good Ulászló, *bene, bene,* gentle and beautiful boy, bloodless king, secret bigamist, happy possessor of Beatrices, Barbaras, Biancas and selected other beauties, with your dear white parrot on your wrist, what would you say to all this?)

Thus evolved the latest product of Bishop Szuhay's proud ingenuity. But perhaps he did not know that most final decisions are made behind clerics' backs, or at most are pulled out from under their feet?

The truth was that the hardworking members of the Prague Treasury - under the innocent title *extraordinary hearing* - were preparing for extraordinary jurisdiction. Of all the possible forums this was the most dangerous - this *judicium extraordinarium* as it was called - but for the present no one in the Archduchy of Vienna would say a word of protest. The accused trembled to hear of it, the reluctant judges were frightened, as the saying goes, to the depths of their souls, but for the time being shunted their fear aside, the depths of their souls being less important than their strategic plans!

Therefore it was absolutely astonishing that it began to be rumoured naively and wrongly in Prague, despite the Judicial Council's proposal and all the accused's humble appeals, that of course if it is "extraordinary", then let it be "extraordinary", though if it's not a private audience, but a tribunal...what's the difference? They did not understand it. The Emperor is overwhelmed by important affairs of state, the petitioner would have to wait a long time; this way he is dealt with immediately. He can say all he has to before the judges, this exceptional tribunal will do nothing other than try the accused in the name of His Majesty... No more deliberate provocation? Capriciousness? Splitting of hairs? The accused could appeal for parliamentary jurisdiction as much as he wanted, but Rudolf just shrugged his shoulders and blinked his little swollen eyes uncomprehendingly. He was merely doing what Illésházy had asked him, what the Council had proposed, was he not?

But in the letter he wrote to his brother there

were no legal or literary niceties, nothing warped, distorted or devilishly demagogic, just the bare facts: "Illésházy's punishment will help the present financial crisis more than a little..." And he touched on, subtly broached (the surface of virgin snow could not have been finer) the fact that other trials would also be necessary to satisfy this need. Inflation, depreciation, all dictated it.

Archduke Mátyás summoned Thurzó and showed him the letter, so ominous and enlightening. One glance (which froze the eyes) was all that was allowed: the lacy ducal cuffs swept and overshadowed the paper, while with his finger he confirmed, lightly touching the lines (a right royal hoax).

At first Thurzó choked, then in an increasingly loud voice he commented on the probable consequences. He spoke of monarchism making a mockery of itself, of the vanity it displayed; but the Archduke interrupted, saying there was no need to go so far...

"It's absolutely necessary," replied Thurzó and continued, would have continued, his tirade against injustice and his growing fear. But the Archduke flung out his arms, as if to embrace the other, saying, this is how it is, that's life, as if he himself were included... (At another time it might have been just the reverse: to embrace but not to declare...or the two together, why not? if one is already up to one's neck in hypocrisy...)

"The people's loyalty will collapse," Thurzó said softly, catching his foot on a corner of the purple velvet rug.

This little pig went to market, this little pig stayed home, this little pig had roast beef, this little pig had none and this little pig cried wee wee wee all the way home...

The old boil of Hapsburg devotion was lanced beautifully.

One by one every member of the Judicial Council received a summons to the "extraordinary tribunal". It comes as no surprise who also received confidential letters, well in advance and bearing Rudolf's signature, in which - along with a stream of terrible threats - they were clearly informed that they must charge the accused of the crime of disloyalty and treason and that he must forfeit both his head and his property.

The unorthodox nature of the proceedings was now no longer hidden behind net curtains or grass screens. The name of the tribunal: *privatum judicium.* The councillors had asked for something *private,* and if the term *extraordinary* unnerved them, let it be to their own taste! Everyone gets the concessions they deserve.

The date of the hearing was set for February the twenty-fifth, 1603. It was not accidental. The opening of the trial was to fall just at a time when the accused's unwanted protector, the Archduke, was to travel to an Imperial gathering. A good distance away.

But at the appointed time neither the judges nor the president of the court appeared.

Did that mean...?

I am afraid not.

They simply had not received their travelling expenses, although these had been promised to them.

But that (if necessary) was easy to remedy.

Their travelling expenses duly pocketed (liberal amounts of it), the judges straggled to the scene of the trial...

21

And then there came trouble. ("Send word if there is trouble...").

According to unanimous depositions taken at a later date, it was during the winter of 1603 that the first signs of madness were detected in Susanna Forgách, the first, revealing flutterings of mania.

That is, those who saw it believed it to be so.

The sun had risen, but was still struggling against the clouds (except for the highest peaks, the faraway, mysterious burning snowcaps). Susanna went out barefoot into the cold corridor. She stepped onto the retreating, wan and ragged sun-rays, as if she believed these weak, narrow beams could warm her soles. Her night-gown was loosely wrapped about her and the free play of fasteners and tapes revealed her long thighs at every step. Her hair, like a Madonna's, hung loose on her shoulders, the untrained curls and tresses swinging rhythmically at every step.

Whomever she met she stopped and informed, in the most perplexing way, as if it concerned the inhabitants of that house, that "Lord Bakics has gone to Rome to arrange to take me for his wife..."

But (a tiny hair in the sweet soup of love) everybody knew that Peter Bakics had only gone to the neighbouring cattle market. If anyone dared to remind her that such things are not so simple, she smiled mysteriously.

Often, in the dark of the night, she roamed about, waking whom she could, so that they would help her, quickly, to brew tea, powder or whatever was necessary to make her sleep. Even in her dreams, if she finally somehow dropped to sleep, Lord Bakics stood beside her bed and woke her, tickling her, repeating again and again, *"Noscitur adverso tempore verus amor..."* (that is to say: In misfortune you will see what true love is - so explained Susanna to her serving maids, who certainly did not understand Latin). Then, "Wake up! Wake up!" and again the Latin words, with little pauses between them, beautifully articulately while Bakics caressed her body, at every word a different place.

As he said *noscitur* he touched her forehead, *adverso,* her nose and mouth, at *tempore* he touched the back of her neck, at *verus* he turned to the valley where the two hills of her breasts met, and *amor*? What could *amor* signify?

One might ask, was this not quite enough for Ferenc Révay?

Later the astonished lawyer would also ask him this, noting certain inconsistencies in the case documents. Ferenc's reply: "I trusted him, my attention was elsewhere..."

"Why did you not know sooner?"

"Because if there had been something between them, she would have kept quiet about it. At least so I thought in my stupid cuckoldry."

Well...yes and no.

These familiar, rational conclusions led to a logical dead-end.

The senses reveal clearly what the forced pace of our hunted days anaesthetises.

During that winter Ferenc Révay's behaviour also altered strangely.

Like one who would finally take possession, if not of the house itself, then of the grounds, he became extraordinarily forward with his wife. Not aggressively, but rather in a calculated and almost ingratiating way, like a man who stakes everything on one last, bogus card.

Now he was weighed down with awkward courtesies, as if he were following a recipe only known from hearsay (the ideal marriage copied out by hand from a Chinese cookbook?), as if his wife were on loan. At every opportunity he would praise or only slightly criticise Susanna's clothes, all in a playful and jovial way: "That skirt is beautiful, but yesterday's was more so!" or the reverse, "Yesterday's was also beautiful, but see how much better this one goes with the colour of your hair..." Or another time, "You look tired...you must have slept badly. Did the full moon upset you?" He would ask such questions ten times with great persistency.

He followed his wife around constantly. But this show of attending on her only increased the distance between them. For Susanna his old reserve had concealed some latent possibility. Now, however, she only had one aim, to get away from him. She was, to say the least, desperate and despondent.

Show is used deliberately here, along with the picturesque *attend.* For he who had always hidden everything now expressly sought notice from an audience.

And so it happened one day, just as lunch was being served. Susanna was not yet sitting at the table (she was normally the last to arrive), but the rustle of her skirts awoke some blind hope in Ferenc Révay, who stood up, rushed towards her and put his arm about her waist (the first time ever). He might have pressed her to him and even embraced her; but Susanna roughly pushed away his indiscreet hand, or rather, flicked him off as one would ashes or bird droppings.

His answering slap danced out from behind the wings of his soul so unexpectedly (and with such force) that afterwards everybody who witnessed it felt they had not "really" seen anything, that their senses had abandoned them just at the moment when the action had occurred.

Susanna ran out - crying, naturally. Ferenc Révay

shoved the door open after her (a stove is usually shoved like this, but sometimes the embers spill out) and began to explain to the assembled others (those in the castle who ate with them) - in a whining, trembling voice not characteristic of him - saying, "Now you have seen the gratitude I get for all my kind words, my sweet, my dear, my dove, my little bug, my star, my beauty, my little fairy, my angel, my little girl, my saint, my jewel, my joy! All these have I called her, I have lavished affection on her. Lace robes? Velvet skirts? Silk sheets? Golden earrings? Musk oil from distant lands? A grey horse? Pomegranates? Did I refuse her anything? What more can she want, I ask you?"

He raised his eyes to the rafters and added unexpectedly: "And if I have no heir, it is not my fault, believe me!"

For a moment he was himself amazed by his own treachery - the words had broken off from their roots and run wild. His head swam. Anxiously he scanned the room. He could not decide (how could he?) whether they were laughing secretly at him or taking his side, because the key thing he knew not: had they guessed something about the secret, the thorn, the hidden wound of his life?

But the listeners, who were without exception servants and underlings, just nodded silently and after a pause attended to their soup, taking care not to let the spoons clink against the sides of the bowls.

Ferenc left his lunch and went after Susanna. He knocked on his wife's door (when she could, she shut herself up in her bedchamber, or at least during the coldest days, as they heated only one room). Then he went in. He watched her silently to see what she would do. (Susanna nowadays read much and with pleasure, welcoming the wise foresight of serious books. Ferenc Forgách, the bishop, sent them in abundance.)

Ferenc Révay sat down and began, as before, "I wish

to speak to you."

But now he knew how to continue - the first fight, it seemed, had from this point of view brought about an improvement. The words welled within him freely, spontaneously, clusters of vague, swaying, unripe intentions. His volubility filled him with sensual feelings.

He went on, we must talk, we must begin all over again, *tabula rasa,* only you must want it, you must believe in it, if you have the strength for it, I have, I know perfectly well that I alone was at fault, I was afraid of you, I was cowardly, it was stupid, I confess, if you can forgive me, perhaps it is not too late, you have suffered, but I too am unhappy...

And all this was said as a matter of course, quite naturally; fair play and no favour, he summoned up all the old recommended maxims, the creative powers of conversation which were suddenly at his disposal.

As if there were not four long years behind them...

He wanted to go on speaking.

But the struggling words fell on deaf ears.

Susanna looked up from her book, exhausted.

Perhaps, she said, it would be better if Ferenc Révay left her in peace...once and for all.

The man stood up, his smile at that moment looked like the old smile when he used to ask her, Susanna, whether or not to heat the rooms, and she would naively reply that she would like...

If that's what you want, he said, snatching the book out of her hands. Susanna shielded her face, or at least tried to.

He struck her many times.

The next day he went kneeling before her, with his sick man's burning eyes, softly calling out "my Susanna", even "my sweet Susanna", because strangely (is it really so strange?), since the first wild assault he, who had always spoken to his wife in the most formal, polite manner, had taken to these simpering and over-familiar forms of address; he accumulated and interchanged them; he was imploring, beseeching, his eyes clouded with tears, oblivious as a Pharisee; he stammered, oozing with sweetness; he was submissive and disingenuous, sometimes one, sometimes the other.

On another occasion he loitered about in front of her locked door, in the dimly-lit corridor, begging for forgiveness...

One can guess the result, and even he was certain that he would never again receive forgiveness from that bedchamber.

Yet sometimes Susanna would gladly have said something to relieve and calm him. For her, compassion and self-pity were bound up in her sense of an oppressive common fate for both of them... I forgive you. Everything is all right, let us forget... But then he would begin again, I want to talk to you, we must speak... Thus she was silent, she withdrew.

For Ferenc, every resort to bended knee, every wave of the *mea culpa* banner, only ended in another paroxysm of rage.

This phase came to an end towards the middle of winter. All the burning resources of his soul ran out.

Then the second phase began. Whatever happened in the castle, a broken pot, a spoilt meal, a lost letter, was blamed on Susanna The most painful thing was not the accusation itself, but her husband's new, pedantic manner. He would reproach her for her sins; saying that she took no care of things, she just gazed into the mirror, that she had changed so much. Once he added that she had grown stupid.

She just cupped her hands over her ears and hid behind her palms (so small children believe that if they see no one, no one can see them...).

At first the man would try to pull her hands from her

face. Then he would sweep things off the table, playing merry havoc with hair brushes, jewellery, jars, belts and clasps; he would watch delightedly as the pearls scattered on the floor. Once he tossed scraps of a ripped silk belt into the air like confetti; another time he snatched the clothes out of the wardrobes and chests, stamping on them with muddy boots.

Susanna tried to save at least her mother's treasures...

She hid in her den like a sick animal. She neglected herself, her hair was often matted, rings appeared under her eyes and her skin erupted; the stigma of despair appeared one by one. She sent a letter asking Peter Bakics for help, to come quickly, as he had promised...to no avail.

Perhaps the letter did not reach him.

Peter Révay did not come their way for Christmas either, because Maria was either pregnant again or already confined. Ferenc's brother just sent a letter in which he confirmed what Peter Bakics had said about further trials in the autumn. But he, Peter Révay, could not believe, or so he wrote, that it was primarily they, the Protestants and Northern Hungarians, who were in danger. He had never been one for false alarms and scares ("We can trust the Archduke implicitly, and our friendship is our security...").

Ferenc Révay had neglected many of his obligations that winter. (Let us not dwell on them! The toils of the seasons are not directly relevant - perhaps precisely because they are otherwise the essential, determining factors.) He who normally carried out the duties of his rank and his landed estates in a detached, but thorough way, made plans to travel after reading his brother's letter. When the weather permitted, he would set out immediately for Vienna, to visit Peter Révay.

We may note the interesting explanation which witnesses later offered for Ferenc Révay's behaviour: "The high and mighty lived in such fear and were so suspicious at that time, they thought it better to be on guard - for what was left unsaid could also be used against you..."

As Ferenc Révay had dissimulated in his private life, so now he turned his face to Prague and Vienna. Ever seeking to minimise, to smooth the provoking surfaces of things, to make them disappear as much as possible... Many others tried to do the same.

They could never believe that their fear of being falsely accused would actually result in punishment and self-punishment, in flight and the endless, fruitless turn of the treadmill, no indeed!

Now even the modest ceremonies of the spirit became official territory.

22

Once again the foaming, icy streams bubbled down from the mountains, racing down the gentle slopes to the plain. In the gardens the scent of spring bonfires mingled with the smell of spring earth. In the castle, windows were flung open. And the long-awaited Peter Bakics arrived.

Ferenc Révay was already on his way to Vienna. Both men had set out with the first thaw - luckily or unluckily? (the fundamental question of our romance!) - in opposite directions.

"When the captain of the garrison declared that horses were approaching, Lord Bakics' horses, and that he was indeed one of the company, the young Mistress almost lost her reason. She ran to the outer gate. Then terrible truth was revealed to him, how yellow her face was, like sad death, so strange a colour, the colour of the shirt she wore - that sort of colour, I remember (clearly the poor man did not like this shirt). The gentleman was startled, greatly shocked by our Mistress' appearance. But he loved her even so, very much. When he clasped her to him, her feet didn't touch the ground. I remember that he didn't kiss her face, but the little valleys behind her ear-lobes; and I can honestly say, I swear on the Holy Bible, that they were so terribly beautiful those two, as they went slowly up the hill in the blood-red light of the sunset, so captivated by each other, so forgetful of everything around them, that as I watched them go my whole being shivered for our poor Master. Heaven and Hell know what rough and stony paths awaited him..."

The eye-witness trembled, understandably.

Charme macabre. Plenty of it. (*Dance macabre,* "dance of death", why not "charm of death"?)

They went on up the hill between the multi-coloured wall of flowering shrubs, not hurrying, for every living moment was certain to thrill and delight, and the next and the next...(and is this not indeed the *differentia specifica* in defining happiness?).

But even so she had to ask: "Why didn't you come sooner?"

"I'm rebuilding Detreko," he replied, whispered in her ear, thus in the present tense - the evasive present. An explanation? Or rather a hidden promise? Though Peter Bakics often talked about this dilapidated, crumbling feudal outpost, his impregnable eyrie; he now mentioned it as if these two, his late arrival and his future plans, were necessarily bound together...(fitting like Russian dolls one inside the other). Perhaps, perhaps he thought that mentioning the castle - even then - would sow the seeds of their freedom, the final yes/no, the last - affirmative - straw? Perhaps.

However, when Susanna explained that Ferenc Révay had left and would not be at home that evening, the man stopped short. He stood for a moment, his look becoming strange, contemplative, lost, even a little startled (he shuddered in the still, gentle air).

Yes, Susanna had at last enlightened him; and this simple fact lit up their whole situation, presenting it like a bright white invitation: *Madame et Monsieur, vous êtes invités...* As if the absent husband was playing a slippery game with them; he held the cards, dealt the hand, but had left the outcome of the game to them alone. So sound the retreat for every sweet suffering, and herald every stolen joy!

Peter Bakics mused, pulling leaves off the budding bushes. He who always hurled himself forward in a passionate encounter with life's unanswered questions, was now at a crossroads, face to face with two doors on which were written "choose". He hesitated, yes or no? As you like it? (Oh, if things were only that simple!) This turn of fortune's wheel disoriented his soul to its very depths.

Susanna, however, put her arms around him and talked, talked and complained that she did not know how she had borne this dreadful winter, that sometimes when the snow had blown through the windows, she had considered running away or killing herself by drinking the sap of poisonous plants, or throwing herself onto the mercy of the rocks, becoming one with the flowers and the earth, dreaming in the depths of the woods, any way she could.

They reached her room (we must not forget to say that they finally went into the house, but how far in...). Peter Bakics embraced Susanna. He drew her to him, and there behind the closed door he opened his heart to her, kissing her, only letting her go for a moment to say "I missed you so much!" and kissing her again wildly. Wildly yet tenderly...(this enigmatic and mysterious duality was his chief strength and virtue.)

It slowly came out - they had to stop kissing for a moment (or perhaps not...) - and Susanna opened the cupboard doors and pulled everything out, all the paraphernalia (the havoc she had reconstructed compared well to the original): unhinged chest-lids, broken locks, handfuls of hair, ripped silk belts, the empty spines of books (threads hanging out of them like raw nerves). Then there were her partly healed wounds, the yellowing lilacs of her bruises, their ripe petals the seals of her peeling scabs. She showed him everything!

But strangely, when she told Peter Bakics of the tortures she had been through, exactly as they had happened, she felt the only thing she could not recall of the whole woeful story was the pain. Somehow everything became light as air and slipped through her fingers, as if all the feelings of pain and fear had congested and evaporated in the filter of that joyous moment - only disembodied words remained. The man listened to her speech aghast, asking over and over, why had Ferenc Révay done this, why, why, why?

Susanna said simply that her husband blamed her for this, that and the other, for every stupid little thing. Meanwhile Bakics stood horrified, picking things up and putting them down again. He might at least have kissed her wounds to alleviate the horror.

Then they had supper. Susanna, who was not eating, just looked at the man. It was good, it was wonderfully good to watch him as he cut the meat, tore the bread, pensive and sober. When he finished his meal, he carefully wiped his mouth, thanked her for supper and kissed Susanna again (as if all he wanted to express was the most formal politeness...).

This charged yet reserved atmosphere affected Susanna (of course the charge in the air was understandable, but the man's reserve was new and strange...).

They looked at each other in wonderment, as if

meeting for the first time.

They began to play cards. They lost themselves in the cards as in the old, calm, beautiful days. But they did not light the candles. They allowed the dusk to fall around them.

And when they could no longer identify the cards, only their outlines and the angles of the furniture, the pale contours of bodies and the lights of the eyes, Peter Bakics took Susanna Forgách's hand - the cards were now definitely on the table - and pressed the damp shells of her palms to his face.

She must understand, he had to leave.

And he was serious. But Susanna simply said, I love you.

He felt exactly the same, but even so. Peter Bakics was bound in honour to Ferenc Révay.

But that is *why* he should not leave her, said Susanna. She went on that her marriage with Ferenc Révay was not a real marriage, that nothing had ever happened between them, nothing in the world...

The spell was broken, and the wind changed.

The man clutched his head, his eyes wide with astonishment. He broke off his musing, shed his reserve and plagued her with questions.

"What do you mean?"

"Simply that." What other details were necessary to tell the tale of this (*lapsus calami*) worthless marriage?

"Never? Not even later?"

"Never, not even once..." Susanna repeated it proudly, almost boastfully; it affected her strangely, although this was understandable.

"So that's why he beats you," said the man, when he had seen the whole book of shame, and had as soon wearied of it. Then he nearly laughed aloud at his perception, combining as it did the most trivial and most profound understanding of events. He had stammered out his faltering *eureka!* From now on his actions would carry his conscience's stamp of approval.

Susanna shrugged her shoulders: Perhaps, perhaps that is why.

Bakics, however, still thought of Ferenc Révay; this new ray of truth did not destroy the pity he felt towards him. He was filled with an overwhelming, universal despair - it was as if the bell tolled for both of them, now that everything was understood. This surge of shame and desperation was coupled with a wonderful tenderness for Susanna - and a sense of relief as well, of course. But then, if he looked at it from the opposite point of view, he felt just the reverse... It was inexplicable.

Susanna had started to speak again about the musician, saying that he had been very sweet, only Maria had detested him. That he had had one blind eye, but this had not bothered her.

That once a bat had strayed into the knights' hall, but they had not been able to catch it.

"So you loved him before me?" interrupted the man, perceiving the sister's trick, the tortuous chronicle of blind eyes and bat catching, the web of rumours. Hidden in his voice was a certain sadness. As if he might still escape her.

"No indeed, my love," Susanna was indignant, adding that, as God was her witness, nothing had happened between them...

Peter Bakics smiled and sighed heavily. The unexpected relief he experienced was not because of what she had said, but the way that she had said it. Perhaps it was her childish optimism, her trusting naivety, her joyous belief in the strength of their love, that brought the man to his knees, so that he delivered himself up to her.

Susanna went on, adding that her whole sad life would have been nothing more than a huge mistake, an unremitting blunder if on that clear, century-turning night he, Peter Bakics, had not arrived, unexpectedly and soaked quite through. If there, in that narrow window niche, in the waxen moonlight under the waning stars, she had not stood in his commanding presence, and he had not looked at her with that pleading, yet possessive, roguish look...

(We might say that "possessive and pleading" come under one hat - under the hat of the mischievous leading characteristic of our leading man - but exactly what is this "one hat"? Isn't it precisely the manifestation of basic human nature? There was a feeble light in his eye which was usually full of invitation and possession - perhaps we simply use or abuse the *carta bianca* of devotion, and that is the source of our imaginings.)

"I didn't know I looked at you like that," he teased; but the teasing was only to disguise his true emotion. He kissed Susanna's palm and finally said, for the first time and very quietly, "I love you."

"I must, if I'm to take the place of your musician...ha ha!" he smiled and slid his hand down the length of Susanna's arm, under the light fabric of her sleeve.

But Susanna said he should have no fear of that, dismissing the musician as if she had never shed bitter tears after Cyprian's departure; while Peter, who sensed this was both a farewell and a memorial to Cyprian, and who was kneeling beside her, simply pulled off her shoes ("never put your shoes on the bed").

He took them off most neatly, then with surprising skill undid the diminutive buttons, ribbons, stockings, the outer and under skirts. He also lit the candles: "I want to see you!" He undressed himself quickly, carelessly, throwing his unbuttoned clothes to the floor in a heap. He watched Susanna, her white nakedness carved in a golden age, softly light up the darkness. Among the unformed masses of shadow, he adoringly, trustingly, sought her out.

First he kissed one breast, "now the other one"; and as
he spoke descended the lower slope of her stomach - the
rhythm of the sentence informed the light, downward,
moth-like rhythm of his grazing - and he knew that he,
Peter Bakics, was the luckiest man in the world! (No
comment for the present...)

Unexpectedly, he stood up, pushed back the fallen hair
on his forehead, tossed back his head sharply, wildly (it is
interesting that at certain moments a loose lock of hair
can be an incitement to rape and at others means
nothing at all...). He clasped Susanna's hand, pulled it
towards him, quickly, peremptorily, and pressed it to his
genitals. She, however, made a willing and happy pupil.
She could feel the violent erection and its accompanying
wetness; and she clasped it as he clasped her. This lasted
only a few divine moments (prologue), as the man had
been a little precipitate during the first embrace (this
haste was, for him, not in the least usual). He felt driven,
as if he were afraid of something, and his movements
became a little awkward; perhaps this was normal,
because his guiding movements as he put the thing where
it should be were *ab ovo* unavoidably clumsy, as rising
above her outstretched body he blindly entered her. It
was quite funny: the pain she felt, if any (myths, myths...)
dissolved in rapture.

Susanna always remembered this first coupling as a
celebration of the soul.

But at that moment the physical act, the wild, fugitive
possession-taking, entranced her. Then she saw for the
first time and with great joy (like looking at the sea from
great height) the other face of man, turned inwards,
submerged into itself when in the last wave of their love a
great and profound solitude descended on her man. Must
a veil be drawn over such moments? This final distance,
this loneliness, she wanted to see it again and again, if
only because its counterpoint was tenderness and devo-

tion. We now accept this withdrawal into the self (*solitude orgastique,* carnal solitude, to be a little more refined) as a biological phenomenon. But lovers through the ages have determined, to no avail, to look into each other's eyes at that moment - a mistake. This withdrawal into the self - precisely because it is uncontrollable - is the most revealing, spontaneous moment... In aftertimes Susanna would try to preserve (though with difficulty) her own gentle meditative state in the midst of the quickening rhythm of their love-making, so that in the final, self-imparting moment she could be participant and witness.

For three whole days they did not put their noses outside the bedchamber.

Perhaps just once. Before dawn Peter Bakics woke up; he wanted to transfer his things into his own room (the guest chamber), but Susanna pulled him back. She could not bear to be separated from him, no matter how briefly. Besides, she had thought up a plan: she would tell the servants she was ill, weak, not to be disturbed, her dear relation would nurse her during the day, no need to say anything more, only that she must rest, and would they just send up drinks and food on trays...

"The young lady and Lord Bakics showed good appetite during the three days they shut themselves up" (a later testimony).

Susanna Forgách felt weak if she just looked at Peter Bakics' elongated, panther nakedness; she overflowed with tenderness as her hand wandered freely through his raven-black hair. She rested her head on the soft incline of his shoulder; she submitted herself greedily and gladly (most greedily) to the man's caressing hands; she drank in his skin, his neck, the fine sweat of his armpits; she caressed and stroked his smooth breast and hairy flanks; she wondered at the pulsating brownness of his loins (here the skin was softer and browner than elsewhere);

she wondered at the trembling and quivering of his testicles, for hidden in these trembles and quivers were all the mysteries of movement as Peter Bakics sat up or turned on his side. This part was perfectly defenceless and crumpled (like snow sliding down the roof of a house), in strange contradiction to the vaunting and demanding self-confidence, the erect, velvety smoothness of the other when the flimsy net of veins and hairs had disappeared, drawing everything to it (sometimes at the most unexpected moments). The opposites fascinated her; and she was filled with adoration for the black pubic hair, too (ha ha, all modesty has fled...), which steadily decreased towards the navel like climbing pines on a mountain slope. When the sun's retreating rays gave way to the shadows of evening, and the man's black hair coloured rust, Susanna remarked, "It seems you are not really raven..." Peter Bakics just laughed, "Of course not," and his strong arms and muscular thighs again clasped her to him, not allowing her to stir (saying: "it can be done like this too!"). Susanna was happy to consent; had not the apostles preached total subjugation (and practically word for word in this form...)? Afterwards she rolled over on top of the man and they rested, chatted; and Susanna would think: what a miracle! Her sister Maria had probably never experienced anything like this beside the upright Peter Révay. She was filled with passion when his penis distended slowly as he awoke and with tenderness when she saw it withdraw...

He kissed her and called her "little sister" - at this of course they laughed a lot.

Susanna once asked: "If Ferenc Révay had not gone to Vienna, would everything have happened between us as it did?" Peter Bakics caressed her head with his long fingers, played lovingly in her blonde hair. "But he went," he said, smiling.

He would not yield any more on the subject. So they

avoided fragmentary references to their past, as they awoke from their dream-like state to the delicate question of the future.

In Peter Bakics' wandering (and previously peaceful) life, this was the first problem that he knew he would not be able to solve himself. He looked to Ferenc Révay's homecoming with empty bewilderment; he had no wish to talk about it. The only two solutions at hand were to flee or fight, and he dreaded both. As their third day together approached its end, he felt his role in this gentle and fertile land, where life itself was pre-ordained, had been lost forever... And when he finally said aloud, anxiously, though he affected lightness, "What next?" (Why has nobody written about the "What to do now?" part of our revolutions of love?), Susanna shrugged her shoulders and with the same affected, light tone replied, "I have simply been ill in bed!" The man felt completely bewildered and after a short, reflective silence said dreamily that he had never been so happy. And he meant it.

In the shadow of that looming homecoming, however, Peter Bakics was caught helplessly in the age-old trap, to flee or to fight. He was locked up, encircled by an impenetrable web like a devil's net.

The Chain of Betrayal
(History Lesson No.3)

On the appointed day and hour of the hearing the
Judicial Council members gathered in the first floor
assembly rooms of Pozsony Town Hall.

One by one.

Like a florist who adds one flower to another to
create a bouquet, the new colours and types not
merely increasing its size, but actually dressing the
arrangement up in different clothes...

The earlier somebody arrived, the more painful
his position, because he had to keep up a conversation until the numbers were complete. The talk was,
of course, solely on the subject most distressing and
worrying for everybody, which even in this closed
circle no one could broach honestly.

Especially since the fanatic Szuhay, the Treasury's
spokesman, had already arrived. And perhaps this is
why he had come first, to prevent any troublesome
tittle-tattle...

Istvánffy, president of the Judicial Council, also
arrived early - for different reasons. His pedantic
nature dictated that he must never be late anywhere, and he always lived up to this, his most
attractive bit of pedantry. Even for something as
completely irregular as this trial (fatally irregular).
During the wait he arranged, tidied and further
annotated his papers with obvious anxiety.

He occupied himself.

Only in order that he should not have to take part

in Szuhay and Joó's jolly conversation.

Seventeen people were present at this, the third sitting of the Judicial Council.

Four stayed away (after the Emperor's very clear letter their excuses were really a sort of discreet opposition).

György Thurzó also excused himself, whether due to moral reflection or a subtle understanding of the future...probably the latter.

Ferenc Nádasdy did not come either, naturally.

But let us take a closer look at the stages in this story of betrayal. Let us see how many of the judges summoned decided to oppose the Emperor's will in the Judicial Council's three consecutive sittings. We will look at the numbers in percentages (unmindful of the probable wrath of the statisticians; because if we dare to practise what we preach, we must not be faint-hearted...).

So here goes...25:60:19. There we have it!

In the first sitting of the Judicial Council nobody took the case seriously, few thought it worth provoking Rudolf's vanity by protesting or staging a boycott... This was the "not worth it..." stage. At the time of the second sitting the true, monstrous visage of the case showed itself, veiled but present; things became serious (but still not bloody), although the danger of a slow expansion of unlawful acts, of a larger infection, now affected everybody. Then the absurd scales of survival tipped in favour of protest. This was the "perhaps it's worth it..." stage.

In the third Council sitting everybody's existence was threatened in black and white unless they turned with downcast eyes to the age-old strategy of submission. Should we call this the "it's not worth it at all..." stage, perhaps? The whole process would make a colourful graph of honour (or its opposite).

It was spring once more. The arrival of spring was testified to by the accumulated, yeasty stench of rubbish in the streets and courtyards.

The judges were sleepy and tired; they complained of lethargy and illness. Through the high windows of the Council Chamber the slanting sun-rays intersected the room, lighting up the dust, the filmy wings of flies, flies and dust in abundance. The hearing was loathe to begin, even after noon. They just sat there, dull-witted fat men in great, deep armchairs.

The judges procrastinated, cast adrift, exchanging innumerable words, shifting and shuffling - as if in this lulling heat their half-muttered, arrogant mumbling would form into a decision which satisfied their hearts and consciences. The old story, that the accused had not committed any crime but was merely defending his legitimate rights, was rehearsed to its limits. But time was running out, beaded brows and sweaty palms were wiped, and by the time the whole picture was coloured, it seemed as if they were truly prepared to defend the accused's innocence... Their spirits rejoiced, really rejoiced, until Szuhay, rising from his chair with a forceful look, turned towards the President of the Court, who was longing to leave, and said:

"Well now, gentlemen, if you are ready, then perhaps we can turn to the matter at hand?"

But then a small loophole presented itself (a blind alley fit only for a mole, really)...

Ferenc Forgách, the bishop (he who had lunched with the Papal Nuncio and dined with the Jesuits before coming hither), reminded them that they should render unto Caesar that which is Ceasar's - Christ himself had urged no less! - but they could not deliver a final judgement, considering that not all were present (this was now the new argument), but merely a written proposal. (The mole is never sure where he is going to emerge...)

So Szuhay took their appeasing Judicial Council "proposal" to Prague (we can be certain that he was not exactly triumphant). He also took Janos Joó with him, who had in the last few weeks clung to the president of the Treasury (like slimy seaweed to a rock).

During his audience with the Emperor, Szuhay added his own advice:

That this case could be a precedent for the rest... That if it proved so easy to sabotage the Emperor's will, and if the punishment was too lenient, then sooner or later the most loyal servants of the Crown would become revenging angels and street corner assassins... Of course it would be no wonder because it seemed that in Vienna and Pozsony they served another king, not their legitimate ruler.

Now *this* mad Rudolf liked! (He simply yawned at the first part...)

The president of the Court and the accused, Istvánffy and Illésházy (almost interchangeable, aren't they?) received practically the same summons at the same time. They were to come to Prague as soon as possible on His Majesty's business! Istvánffy was to bring the Court Seals with him as well...

Für alle Fälle (just in case).

Judge and accused were equally unwilling and reluctant to prepare for this journey, but they set out.

On the night before his departure István Illésházy, the accused, thought of the tasks ahead. After a short attack of bitterness (on the first day of the hearing he had been delighted by their benevolence - what could happen, after all? - they had held out generous hopes...), he carefully assessed who was worth approaching, rousing (we might also add, who was worth lining up against the wall).

He wrote down, in a dozen copies, the same few sentences, "Defend yourselves well in advance, as well as you can, for we are living in an age of deception and sycophancy, and truth has been completely suppressed..." He sent this message to, among others, the Révay brothers. Then he sifted and hid away his letters and papers.

He read until it was dark. He found, for example, the first draft of an old letter which, during a period of friendship and trust, he had written to Janos Joó. In it he had quoted old King Mátyás - perhaps reading the recipient's mind? - who had said that "there are some Hungarians who would consign their souls to hell, in order that they might do more harm...", and that "love grew cold and the whip cracked upon us..." What had prompted him to write thus? He could not remember. But it must have been a truly delicate matter if he had prepared a draft and had even called up the spirit of the great king. Then Illésházy had an idea that rose up from his guts and seeped into his brain.

He hunted for Janos Joó's reply. It rattled about in his brain that something had happened years before, he had a feeling more than a clear recollection, and as he searched for the exchange of letters he was filled with disquiet...

He pulled out what he needed. In his reply Joó had exhorted him not to give up, to speak out even against the Emperor! (What about? It seems they had both known without it being mentioned...) He grumbled that if this went on he too, Janos Joó, would stand with the opposition. He declared he wondered at the world, "because His Majesty does not respect our laws, he does not defend us from the Turks, he betrays our land and squanders our resources, and does not even allow us to defend ourselves..."

The age-old motto of our Hungarian Romance.

And in another letter, "You see that this dynasty is still scourged by God, it is slowly losing all its empire... Believe me, if there were somewhere to go, I would leave the country..."

What is true is true (another tautology...), but István Illésházy had never put anything in writing even if he had thought the same. Now he felt shocked and indignant that such a man would accuse him. All that they levelled at him, all that they sought to brand him with, was nothing compared to this disloyalty! The morsel of undigested falsehood had been retched up. It purged him, so that he felt like an empty room, an echoing chamber in which these iniquitous words resonated with elemental force. He decided to take the letters with him to Prague.

The Emperor's bodyguards were waiting for him at the gates of Prague. Their captain greeted him extremely politely: his accommodation had been arranged with all the respect due to his rank. They accompanied him to a a well-furnished palace and with low bows bade him farewell, saying that he was not to leave his apartments until summoned by the Emperor.

Days passed and nothing happened, while he sat under this comfortable Prague house arrest; his letters were not answered, but all his needs were attended to. Only the silence, the passing, senseless and uneventful days became tortuous; the sense of powerlessness grew hard to bear. But then came a sudden whisper, a tiny gleam of hope, a faint possibility of breaking the silence, of opening the once dumb, but now unstoppable Sibylline mouth of officialdom.

The Treasury officials could only gape: who had ever heard of such indiscretion? They quickly and secretly made copies of the most pernicious parts of Joó's letters. In important palaces, in important rooms (and offices) they brought them out with diffident shakes of the head and helpless titters. (That is what you call playing the hard game of politics.)

The whole affair could either be played down in a patronising manner: "Please come back just a moment! He would like to see you..." (Of course he would!) Or approached in a fawning and cautious way: "Have you seen His Eminence yet...?" (He could not really read them properly because his anger was so great that...) Another question: Who would have the last laugh, he who revealed them, or those to whom they were revealed...?

Then someone opined that he knew the person who wrote these letters had always been a traitor. He had a nose for such things and had sensed Janos Joó's unreliability (though he had chosen to remain silent and merely keep on his guard). Of course someone else immediately seconded, yes, that's right, don't you remember, *Meine Herren,* that apparently small incident when the "letter-writing gentleman" dissuaded the Hungarian aristocracy from staging a grand reception for our Hapsburg Crown Prince by arguing it was not worth the expense? At the time we dismissed it, naturally. But recollections such as this would not do any harm, would they?

So they rummaged in the black bag of gossip and blunders which had accumulated over the years. No, it certainly could not hurt.

A secret investigation was initiated against Janos Joó.

Illésházy was not informed of these developments, of course. But, as if to appease him, the first replies to his petition arrived. Still, one swallow does not make a summer.

Meanwhile the Council's "proposal" (one swallow, two swallows...the whole flock would not have been enough to oppose it) had been copied by diligent hands onto a new document; it had been smartened up and back-dated, turning it into a formal sentence. It is strange that when this apocryphal document was ready, all trace of the original was lost forever. Was it destroyed? The tendency of autocracies to immortalise themselves is well known (in brown, in red, it is all the same), thus it was probably not destroyed. It was more likely lost and disintegrated while it was being transcribed and falsified, not to be found even when the strictly-guarded iron chests, the mammoth, padlocked cupboards were stripped bare by history (to make room for others...).

The sentence now lacked only the signature and seal of the president of the Court.

Not for long.

Remember: *für alle Fälle...*

The Imperial officials found Istvánffy easy to manage, especially when they cast their thoughts over all his previous prevarications, life-saving rhetoric and faithful stands.

How was it done?

With the most ancient method of persuasion, I'm afraid.

Did Istvánffy hold the reproachful seal with downcast eyes and trembling hands?

He was, above all, disputatious.

The president of the Court even extorted a modest sum, arguing, "Please look into it if you want, but any lawyer would ask at least ten thousand forints for this work...; he would expect damages for making his soul ache so much from this betrayal."

Time flew by, the summer ended, but enough! On a late autumn day, when the black, slippery mucous of fallen leaves was heaped up in the streets of the Imperial City, it transpired that the execution of István Illésházy's death sentence had been transferred from Prague to Vienna - so successful had the Archduke's heartfelt intercession been with his brother.

The accused could travel there freely, because Bishop Ferenc Forgách had undertaken to accompany him to his Viennese prison. That far-sighted Ferenc Forgách, that church-abiding vanguard of the Counter-Reformation (less than a year to go) now willingly stood beside the Protestant lord. (It often happens that way...)

The bishop bid him farewell by the Vienna city gates.

"You can find the way by yourself," he said to Illésházy, and squeezed his arm.

But István Illésházy did not go to the dungeons; instead he went straight to his loyal, old friend Ferenc Nádasdy (Annagasse, the third building on the left, still to be seen today, the Hotel Schweizerhof).

It was All Soul's Day. Hysterical winds bent the branches of the trees, scattered the fallen leaves, swung the bushes, drummed the rain on the windows of the houses, and blew up Illésházy's cloak as he got out of the carriage under the arch of the gate. "I'm wet through!" No matter, he was free, laughed Ferenc Nádasdy as he embraced his guest. The joy of meeting again brought tears to their eyes.

The celebration of male friendship and loyalty was only marred when Illésházy's tale reached the tiny but worldly episode about the letters: an angel passed overhead. They drew the curtains, and Nádasdy's special guard were stationed at all the entrances to the palace. They awaited Archduke Mátyás that evening, strictly *incognito.* The Archduke's unique hawkish profile was covered by a Spanish hat pulled well down. He stayed only half an hour, not even time to finish his supper. He advised Illésházy to leave for Poland...

On the following morning the Judicial Council's fourth and now final sitting was opened with bored and rapid words.

Their completely formal, sanctioned (with unholy, sanctimonious sanctioning), half-hearted, and bell-tolling final round was, by this time, being dragged on by only a few in the Council.

Janos Joó, who was still a member, tried to explain to Ferenc Forgách - who naively pressed to commute the beheading - that mercy would be inappropriate. The bishop only once replied, "There is the estate, so what need of the head?" Janos Joó mumbled about precedents and pontificated with bearded wisdom; but Ferenc Forgách kept on fixing him with a strange, distant smile which finally numbed his words. Perhaps he understood the meaning of this smile the next morning when the arrests were made, and the heavy soldiers' boots stamped across his bedchamber...

The president, Istvánffy, would later try to salvage something from Joó's sequestered chattels. (He was not successful.)

While the iron doors were closing behind Janos

Joó, the Archduke's henchmen in Vienna were also rushing to Nádasdy's palace, but they found no trace - need we say more? - of Illésházy. They swept through the city, causing a furore, a deliberate uproar rather like a draught slamming the door behind you. Sleepers were awakened from their dreams and wondered with rheumy eyes at this excessive clattering... On the Archduke's orders, they pulled up and then let down the city gates. The rusty grids creaked and clanked.

The central character in this false and shameful episode had left all that behind him and was closer by then to the end of his forced journey than to any pursuer. As he reached the border, he may have stopped for a moment and even looked round with new eyes. Ahead lay fields covered with the first light snowfall, like a table laid with cups brimful of freedom or strange objects of mystery.

Or perhaps not?

Perhaps it was only the negation of negation...

23

Ferenc Révay did not find his brother in Vienna. Peter Révay had already set out for Holics Castle.

In his disappointment (possibly he was not that disappointed), he fairly shrank from the court and other high company. He walked through Vienna's streets, squares and alleys, familiar from his school days, and was reminded of the long-bearded, rabbinical wise man who supposedly understood dreams. He remembered the house. It was in one of the tiny streets of the Jewish quarter, where the crumbling walls twisted and crowded together, blocking out all but a narrow strip of the sky.

With great reverence the man led Ferenc Révay into his back room, a sanctuary crammed with holy books (the front was the preserve of a modest draper's). The advance of the years was only shown in the changed colours of his beard, in its rusty brown and pale white lights. He had never looked young when he was young, and now he did not look old although he was fairly advanced in years.

Ferenc Révay explained that recently he had had a recurring dream in which nothing seemingly personal or important happened. The scene was confused, loud and tumultuous, as many people tried to free a wonderfully worked, gilded and lacquered coach from the mire. Each strenuous pull was accompanied by drum rolls, or to be more precise, for every push and shove there was a vague thud, so that eventually one regulated the other. The drummer was hidden behind a tree, his face could not really be seen, but the instrument was remarkable, it was huge, with long, gold tassels dangling around it. But all the effort was in vain. Every show of strength just broke another ornamental piece off the coach; the wheels would not budge.

Ferenc Révay's first question was why did he, the dreamer, have no part in the dream.

"Because, Sir, you are everything in the dream. You are the mud, you are the coach, and you are also the people who want to free the coach.

"One must change one's point of view, shift one's gaze, just as the centuries alternate in the different regions of the world.

"If you like, you are the mud, your soul is formed from mud, from slippery earth, from barren earth which devours and binds those who would like to run, to be born along on their way in beauty and with light wheels.

"If you like, you are the coach, precious, valuable and unique, but bound by the mud. Every effort to break free just loses you another piece.

"Finally if you like, you are all the observers, even the flying birds who look down on the earth. You would like to help yourself, to pull yourself from the mire, even by the roots of your hair, but that is not possible. The more you desire it, the more damage you will do to the coach..."

"And the drum?"

"Would you allow me to take your hand for a moment?"

Ferenc Révay held out his right hand.

"Now please give me the other one."

With cold fingers the man decorously placed Ferenc's right hand on his own left wrist, on his pulse.

"Do you hear the drum now, Sir?"

They were silent.

"What is the answer?" asked Ferenc Révay. Perhaps this dream sequence would come to an end before long, but he felt a great burden weighing him down, a great tiredness.

The man smiled, or rather it was as if the smile radiated from the great deep rings under his eyes, the fan-shaped wrinkles and folds, as if his whole face smiled without his lips moving, and his whole being seemed wrapped in this radiating smile.

"Perhaps you should not travel in a coach after there has been rain... But perhaps it has already happened?" and he stretched out his arms, or rather his hands, palms outward, and his eyes went on smiling.

Ferenc fled. He did not feel at all angry at the bearded man's strange methods (perhaps sensing the irrevocability of God's creations...).

He fled as if pursued by the devil.

Ferenc Révay decided to return home via Holics. He now desired Maria's company, he would tell her every-thing, he would release the rush of words festering within him. He could entrust himself to Maria, to her sound principles, to her cool hands, to the strength of her well-ordered conventions.

He took presents for the little ones.

But when he finally got there, he just sat beside her, as always, unable to say a word.

"Thank you, I am well, Susanna too. Only, the winter has been tortuously long..."

"And cold," said Maria, and she began to complain. He found his brother in a disturbed mood. Away from home Peter Révay was of a confused disposition; but now that he was with his wife, he was turning double somersaults of shame. He was ashamed of the accused and ashamed of the judges.

"They're starting new trials...," said Peter Révay, so softly that his voice could hardly be heard. "Unfor-tunately," he added, "primarily against us Northern Hungarians and Protestants..."

"And what of, what of 'our brother' Thurzó, what does he think of all this?" Ferenc Révay was extremely interested to know.

"He's very gloomy nowadays," replied Peter Révay, giving his brother an unusually concessive, indeed pleading look, when Ferenc Révay burst out, "That I believe!"

Peter Révay went on to say that Thurzó had not been particularly loquacious, he had just answered Peter's questions about what was happening with: "government requirements".

"Perhaps he was just showing his true colours."

Ferenc turned away, with his brother's voice behind him as he read out Illésházy's letter, with gentle, almost painful, constraint (so, great gentleness follows hysteria). To this Peter added in a pondering, hesitant way, as if he intended it as a small afterthought, a compassionate postscript to assign a fitting place for his shame:

"It seems they're planning to accuse people of incest."

Only later did Ferenc Révay discover, from somebody else, that the one accused of incest was (as it happens...) Tamás Nádasdy, Ferenc Nádasdy's younger brother.

There was only one question left, who would be next. Could it happen to him, too...?

His wealth, his great estates, his Protestant beliefs, the wound, the stigma of his private life could all too easily be ripped open, laid bare to the world...it could happen. In the moments that followed, Ferenc felt incapable of even raising a protest.

On whose side in this are marching the unruly recruits of reason? Can the triumph of base fear and crude self-interest coincide with Reason's much-vaunted conquest of Romanticism? Indeed, the assault on common sense, its enforced exile, its evil perversion occur at just such moments of our Hungarian Romance, when the inconceivable becomes the only thing that makes sense.

What is the root in this, in our creation, that at key moments Reason's two stalwarts - *Sein und Sollen,* what is and what ought to be - never meet?

He might have wrestled with but one thread of this inquiry alone all the way home, but the defeated, philosophising army scattered, were left behind, and a much more practical question arose in his soul: would he have to flee?

<h1 style="text-align:center">24</h1>

The truth was that Ferenc Révay's position on the stage of the *vita publica* was very similar to the hidden quagmire of his *vita privata.*

But could the outer and the inner, the facade and the interior, the role-playing and true belief be reconciled somehow, harmonise with each other?

For a short time, perhaps.

His grandfather, the first Ferenc Révay, belonged to the generation that struggled in the great cataclysm after Mohács (with his brother István), when new faith and illusions of loyalty to the throne aroused a passion for construction and action.

The first Ferenc Révay was a famous Palatine, one of the most outstanding exemplars of the "fathers of nations" - his name and praises of him can be found in several chronicles. They honour his distinguished scholarship, his legal and architectural knowledge, his observant eye, his stoical nature... Emperor Ferdinand appreciated his virtues and bestowed him with gifts, Szklabinya was one such present. But not even he was immune to greater or lesser slights to his self-esteem. It is easy to imagine that this nationally respected Palatine did not feel too comfortable when provocative, arbitrary charges were dangled like puppets before his eyes, which - many could bear witness to it - said that he harboured Zwinglian beliefs about Holy Communion; *ergo,* he was denied membership of the Aulic Council. But the wound healed easily: the charge was virtually inaudible, both the Emperor himself and a Catholic priest sprang to his defence...

It was, after all, an age of experiment.

His son Mihaly, and his brother - there were also two of them, also known as the "two Révays" - actively carried on their father's traditions. They were both on parliamentary committees, planning and haggling over details on the delicate bridge of compromise, treading carefully, while affairs of state advanced not an inch... These illusions of loyalty to the throne began discreetly to crumble when directives from Vienna were thwarted, and many raised their voices openly and loudly in defence of a Hungarian constitution.

The loudest and fiercest among them were the two Révays.

Mihaly Révay rose to speak. He considered the columns in the shadowy chamber, the scattered compatriots who watched him at first animatedly, later disconcertedly, and finally only glancing at him before looking away. Rudolf's neck, crammed between his millstone collar and his grotesquely protruding chin (his doughy chin had a life of its own), stiffened as Mihaly said, "We beseech that under the reign of Your Majesty we will be freed from the oppression, tyranny and slavery of former times!"

Rudolf nodded, his collar crackling at every incline of his head; he did not say a word because his thoughts had long since strayed to his national museum, to his dazzling private picture gallery in the palace, as they always did when he awoke in a melancholic and evasive mood, as he had on that day.

(Later all the symptoms and signs of his madness would become clear - they would require a separate inventory. Then the bragging dictatorship of astrologists, fortune tellers and alchemists at court would weave a tangle of parasitical and limpet-like corruption around the Emperor's person, the disintegrating personality made easy prey.)

However, the Hapsburg Archduke of the time leapt from his chair - until that moment he had seemed so temperate, never twitching a muscle - and accused the Révay brother of endangering the rule of the Germans by such behaviour!

The charge was seen as so patently absurd that at first there was silence. Should they laugh? Take it as a joke?

But nobody laughed.

Mihaly Révay stood up without a word, as if he had been kicked off his chair, and leisurely walked out of the chamber, slamming the door.

But this defiant farewell is not the end of the story.

He had already decided in the all-consuming silence of the Council Chamber that he would never again go anywhere near national government. He had barely arrived home at Szklabinya, recovered his breath and told his wife about the events, when an Imperial messenger arrived, a certain Count Herberstein, who told him to get on his horse or into his coach, as he had been summoned by the Emperor, who wanted a private word with him.

Mihaly would not go one step, never again.

The messenger would have to return to His Majesty without him.

Mihaly Révay would stay.

And so they would stay too. Count Herberstein's one-hundred-strong mounted company camped in the castle.

At first they behaved with perfect correctness. They thanked their hosts for food and drink, kept to their quarters and attended to their needs in the privy.

Count Herberstein presented Mihaly Révay's wife with a fine precious ring: a gift from His Highness.

But Lady Révay ("an awe-inspiring, straight-backed woman...") did not put it on her finger, she locked it in a little box.

One day it would be a wedding present for Maria Forgách, who proudly displayed it, boasting, "they received this gift from the Emperor" - with her nose held high to the moon and her voice simpering.

Mihaly Révay locked himself in his room. He would answer nothing.

In the corridor, where the younger Révay son, Ferenc, stood for hours, all that could be heard was the creaking of the floor, the grating of cupboard doors, the scraping of a chair being moved across the room.

At first the soldiers just peeped into the kitchen, which was awash with good smells. Then they started to raid the larders.

Count Herberstein would periodically stand before the locked door and say, "Talk to your father!" But Ferenc just shook his head.

In a short time the people and horses had eaten everything.

The soldiers danced through the castle, their arms full of cushions, embroidered cushions. They only wanted to rest their heads on them. But when they took over the wine cellar, all hell broke loose in Szklabinya.

They forced the female servants, screaming and wailing, to walk on all fours while they formed a great queue to look up their skirts.

They split the cushions and then the feather mattresses and flung handfuls of feathers out of the windows, shouting, "It's snowing!"

They urinated from the top of the staircase in great arcs.

Count Herberstein apologised, of course, saying he had tried everything. He trod cautiously up the violated stairs, holding the swaying banisters - he was truly sorry for what had happened, but everything depended on Mihaly Révay, on him alone. No one else.

That night Mihaly Révay hanged himself.

His servants cut him down in time.

But when they laid him carefully on the bed, he was still and deathly pale.

Lady Révay (who had earlier fended off the prying Count so that he had to wait in the corridor), opened the door a crack and told him with haggard but dry eyes that death had set in.

Count Herberstein was relieved. He did not stay to see the corpse, but set forth immediately to deliver the news to the Emperor.

In the weeks that followed the older son, Peter, clung to his mother's skirts, terrified, and avoided the sick-room as much as possible.

By contrast Ferenc would not leave the chamber. He listened and listened to his father, who finally blamed God for the abortive scheme of human affairs. The boy listened with burning eyes and bated breath, absorbing all the shackles, signs and realities of humiliation and bitterness.

25

Readers should be warned that in the next scene they may encounter some obscene and offensive material.

Ferenc Révay's arrival was met, not with the usual words of greeting, "Welcome, Sir!" or "How was your journey?" but with "Peter Bakics is here" ...and behind this salutation something unusually provocative and decidedly roguish. He was struck by the voluptuous tone, a certain residue of things unsaid, but that was all; there seemed no reason to dwell on it. In fact he was pleased by Bakics' presence; Ferenc could hardly wait to show his friend Illésházy's warning letter. But he did not want anyone to notice his impatience, so he just said, "Good. First let me settle in".

His naivety in this last moment of ignorance, given the change in his fate, was poignant. (In the museum of Ferenc's memory this moment took on special significance...) As they removed his clothes, brushed his cloak, brought a wash basin for his hands and face, wiped his shoes, the self-appointed messengers began coming forward - fat, black crows of disaster circling and alighting - to prise open their master's eyes with their long beaks...

The first, a certain Janos Kutsera, stuck his head around the door (Peter Bakics had himself brought him along, thinking him a loyal man):

"As the Master was brushing his hair, I decided to come forward. I had spent a whole day struggling with myself, but those two had brought such shame into this guilty world that I must spit it out. The Master just seemed to keep fingering his hair as I told him that the Mistress and my Lord Bakics had shut themselves up for three whole days, that they hadn't even once come out and that the Mistress had apparently slept with him in there. Then the Master turned to me and asked how I could be sure, whether I was not just harbouring some resentment in my heart. So help me God...ask anyone, your honour, I said. Christ's own face on the Cross couldn't have been paler and more bloodless than his face then. But he shouted insults at me and would have struck me if I hadn't run out in time" (Janos Kutsera's testimony before the Supreme Court).

Now Ferenc knew everything, and it was more than he had imputed even to Basirius-Beelzebub himself; that is, almost everything, because the sweetest, most important things that had happened, that cannot be summed up in court casebooks, of these Ferenc Révay naturally had no idea.

He was filled with nausea and horror. But his anger was even greater.

He ran as if the moon were after him.

The two lovers were playing cards again - for a moment, as Ferenc opened the door, he could see their heads bent together. Squat, solid candles burned on the table. Of course they had known of his arrival - their partisans had run to them, too.

Susanna was terrified, but was too ashamed to admit to Peter, that she, who had earlier shrugged her shoulders, was now afraid. Bakics felt just the reverse. Face to face with the inevitable, he was calm and was prepared for the worst (though he did not believe for a moment in opposing Ferenc). Neither did he feel like confiding in Susanna. So, despite appearances, those two were not weaving plots.

Ferenc walked in and stopped still, without saying a word in greeting. Susanna acknowledged him with a trembling, constrained sweetness, her head tilted a little to one side.

By contrast Peter struck up in the most natural manner (without leaving any pauses for thought or for replies), as he poured and offered Ferenc some wine - that he had been very much looking forward to Ferenc's return, so the two of them could have a good conversation together (this might have been true, especially if...).

"I will pour my own wine if I wish to drink," said

Ferenc Révay. This was not, of course, the main question (who poured wine for whom), but the truth was that while his emotions raged within, Ferenc simply could not find words like "I know you have seduced my wife!"

"Why are you angry with me?" asked Peter Bakics, holding the long-stemmed goblet ceremoniously in his hand as if preparing the Stations of the Cross, as if he too had no idea what to say next.

That made it easier.

"Get out of my house."

And Ferenc Révay continued - indeed, he had only just started - convulsively, with the merest pretence at restraint (addressing only the man as if Susanna were not present - he did not look at her once). He clutched a chair: that his trusted friend, his childhood playmate, his dear cousin (it was not clear where this was leading), his close companion, his diligent bearer of news, his solicitous relation, his welcome guest and so on and so on, rambling obsessively, using words he had never uttered before. Peter, in whom he, Ferenc, had stored and shown so much faith had now (who would have believed it?) wormed his way into his peaceful house looking for an opportune moment, wheedling, insinuating, plotting to trick his wife, to put her up against the wall (!) - and with increasing irrationality Ferenc repeated his vulgar and offensive words. Then, as if to punctuate the end of his list of grievances, he smashed the chair, kicking and pushing it under the table and breaking its back. But he had not finished. He went on, "I trust you made good use of my absence, that you didn't waste an hour of the day, morning, noon or night..."

Bakics listened, numb but fascinated. He saw it all as something distant and curious, this spectacle of guilt, this orgy of self-revelation. In his eyes what had happened between him and Susanna was sweet nothing compared to these declarations belched and vomited up in front of him. He did not intend to do anything, but an almost sensual insolence awoke within him.

"Somebody might as well do something," he said, smiling.

Susanna simply watched them, even forgetting to put down the cards, holding them out like a fan. She too was held in a strange inner paralysis as she listened to them, as if she had no part in their lamentable quarrel. The words hummed and chimed in the distance but did not seem to penetrate her calm. She did not move, but - unusually - her eyes clung to every tiny detail; she saw them as she had never seen them before. Susanna watched the men as one watches a sleeping person, a sleeper who exposes the core of his soul, casting off all the outer and salon pretences of daily life. In Peter Bakics she perceived a hitherto unapparent inner uncertainty; he seemed dumbfounded and incapable of action just at the most critical moment (the unique, crystal-clear moment which one must not disturb, or it will crumble to dust in one's fingers). In her husband's combative but flourishing tirade she discovered a frail yet heroic strength that she had never noticed before, even when he had attacked her, or at least not in this expiating sense.

She was roused from her trance by a thud. Her husband had begun shouting "Get out!" again. He pushed the door open, overturning the wineglass, which fell to the floor. But Bakics was stronger and taller; he clutched Ferenc's arm and tried to push him back into a chair. Ferenc hit out at him. Susanna leapt up between them, trying to separate them with her elbows (fairly hopelessly...). Ferenc then let go of Peter Bakics, only to grip his wife by the hair (always clutching at things...). He pulled up her head and struck her on the face. Why did he need to force her head up at such an unnatural angle? Perhaps so he could see the enlarged pupils, the panic spots, the refracted light of pain in her eyes? Susanna cried out for help, but this was entirely unnecessary because Peter Bakics now began to hit out in earnest, and then Ferenc Révay had to release Susanna.

The repellant spectacle now reached its climax.

Susanna fell to the floor, blood pouring out of her nose and mouth in big fat drops, her hair clinging bloodily to her head; she lay on her side, still as a fresco portrait, pale, wax-white in her torn, pastel-coloured clothes. Peter Bakics was punching his rival. Ferenc Révay fell, dashed against the brazier with a metallic clap, slid down the tiled wall and sat hunched on the floor. (It was then he was supposed to have torn his knee. He later pulled up his leg and displayed it to the world, complaining of lameness; although others testified that he limped only when he could be seen.)

Peter Bakics' head swam and the walls lurched (he too had been hit quite forcefully on the head). The three of them were hopelessly entangled, hands locked, legs akimbo, hair matted, gasping - and to crown it all, some accursed horse was whinnying somewhere in the soft night outside.

In the darkness a few tiny, indifferent lights glowed from the distant watch towers.

Peter Bakics lifted Susanna, carried her out and laid her down in her chamber. He woke the serving wench and told her to alert the doctor. Bakics then went back to Ferenc Révay, who was by now sitting at the table, looking stupefied at the cards, which he then swept away with his hand.

Peter Bakics stopped short for a moment, composing himself, and then told Ferenc to believe him, that he, Peter, had for a long time, a very long time done no more than pity Susanna, because he felt there was something wrong with the poor girl...

Just then an idea came to Ferenc Révay, that he

should take Peter's hand, put his life in his hands, tell all, talk to him intimately about the past and the future - but this thought faded away as suddenly as it had come. Instead Ferenc looked up and said, tauntingly, "Oh, the great Samaritan!"

"Things cannot go on like this...," Peter Bakics continued as if he had not heard. (Sometimes the use of the modest pronoun *this* is so much more exact and indicative, just as what is unnamed holds more riches than the most graphic description - which may simply burst like a bubble...)

"Why not?" Ferenc Révay asked, almost insolently.

"Otherwise I will stay here, to look after her...that's why."

"Or else?" nodded Ferenc Révay, and now he was the one who smiled.

He picked the cards up off the floor.

"You will stay here forever, is that what you mean?"

Now it was Peter Bakics who smiled, no, not forever...only until Ferenc Révay guaranteed not to lay a finger on his wife again.

"What sort of guarantee are you thinking of?"

"Something in writing."

Ferenc Révay asked what he would have to write, with the same pretence of indifference.

And then he threw up his head like a wild-eyed horse, and his eyes, which had been pale and listless, flared with excitement, as Peter Bakics repeated emphatically that he must write everything down, "or I will not leave, I will not move an inch..."

Ferenc Révay immediately replied in a new, jarring, heart-rending tone of sheer spite, "Of course, of course, as you wish, stay here, that will be wonderful! Make yourself at home, move here, forever if you like."

He seemed relieved, although this was not the reason for it, not at all. Yet Bakics' last words had unexpectedly revived him, recovered him from his dazed state, and at the same time abated his raging fury, or at least showed him a way out. A weight slipped lightly off his shoulders as it occurred to him that his present situation bore similarities with his father's. He was amused by the thought, even took malicious delight in it. (Is there such a thing as delight in one's own misfortune? Why not?) The shooting pains in his leg subsided, and he felt something inevitable had come to pass. He almost laughed aloud: Count Herberstein was quartered in Szklabinya in the form of his good-hearted, gentle friend Peter Bakics. And, *mutatis mutandis,* he was strangely pleased; he calmed down. Ferenc Révay had found his role.

He eyed Peter Bakics spitefully, scrutinising him in this brand new *mutatis mutandis* way, and said, "Well let's see, what exactly are the terms of this testimonial? Or what shall I call it?" (He posed the question like an adult to an evasive child, "Come, let's see what's in your report!")

Ferenc went on, "Shall we write it now? That would be fine. I'll just get some paper and a pen... How many sheets do I need? Whatever you wish..." He still did not know where this was all going to lead. But he might as well know without further ado what Peter Bakics meant by *everything.*

He sat down at the table, set the cards aside, acted the part and seated himself comfortably - "the handwriting at least must be beautiful..." (He was now immersed in his role!)

"Won't you also sit down?"

Peter Bakics thanked him but said he would stay where he was. He stood near the window, leaning nonchalantly on the bookcase as if only half there. He felt he could not bear this pathetic show any longer. He lifted the curtain a little, like women lifting their skirts on the stairs, and sniffed the darkness on the hills.

"Tomorrow will be a fine day!"

But when Ferenc Révay remarked in answer that then they could certainly go out in the carriage, on horseback, or would he prefer a walk? - Peter felt overwhelmed by a desire to flee, to go back before it was too late to his old, gently rolling life. It was not always peaceful, but at least his adventures were as honourable and untainted as clean linen... As evening overtook them, he yearned to make sly deals, pacts of possession, or to fight, to show great valour and daring in the midst of great danger. But now he thought with longing of carousals, of brief loves, of his gaunt castle of Detreko, of sparkling streams, mossy tree trunks, the southern slopes of the hills, deer spoor on the forest floor, horse races along the hills with his sister Margit. These he loved, and he felt as if life, his life, which was now paraded invitingly before him, had perhaps been irretrievably lost.

Peter started to speak. He dictated slowly, beautifully, articulately.

A TESTIMONY
(List of offences)

I, Ferenc Révay, do swear
before God,
who delivers us from evil
and shame
and damnation,
who is Lord on high,
the means of our salvation,
do swear as Peter Bakics is my witness
that my wife Susanna Forgách,
from the time of our marriage
has been neither sinful nor guilty
but meek and kind,
and this without reason,

for in my barbarity,
my kicks, my lashings,
my strikes to the face (from her nose ran blood
and her face swelled blue),
I made her blood run,
causing me perverse pleasure
both at home and before strangers,
with whips and terrible blows
I nearly killed her.
Although
I lay in wait for her
I sought her out and hunted her down
in vain,
I neither saw
nor heard
nor felt any evil in her,
yet she
I insulted with
terrible, ugly, loathsome, false, mocking
invective and curses and blasphemes
(which I will not recount due to
their loathsomeness),
she,
whose loyalty and pure living
I well know,
and to whose perfection
I will bear witness
till death do us part.
She bore much suffering
silently, with patience,
but if His Holy Majesty
had not proffered our kinsman into our lives,
into her life of many indignities, of weary
bitterness,
perhaps she would have killed herself.
I will reform

my vows, my broken pledges, my evil ways,
regretting
all oppression
to be certain that
I have renounced my dissolute ways.
As testimony
I give this letter
in my own hand,
with my own seal,
before the author of peace,
the above-mentioned kinsman,
and His Holy Majesty
and the Holy Trinity.
I give my oath,
Amen,
that I will do no such
things
until my grave, until my death;
if, however, I should violate my pledge,
let my letter be circulated
without delay to reproach me,
let my wife be divorced from me,
whatever the law.

The more Ferenc wrote, the more he was relieved - he
gladly accepted everything, but he could not take it
seriously. He bid the trump card of a failed life... Thus he
willingly wrote everything down; the more incriminating
the statement, the more it could be denied as exaggerated or plain false... Of only one thing was he frightened:
that the black lie of their marriage would be exposed.

The closing notion, "to divorce", disturbed him. The
word had been said for the first time. It existed within, of
course, but he had dismissed it from his thoughts, it was
far off at the back of his mind - surely there was no
necessity to write it, to place the letters nicely next to

each other. Of all the sensations which had flittered and fluttered across his self-tormenting soul, that one had already been wearisome enough. Indeed he had lived for years with the notion of divorce, since the night of his abortive marriage to be exact. Now the abyss had opened once again at his feet.

"We are finished, now you must sign it," said Peter Bakics.

But Ferenc waited, meditating. Silence now filled the empty spaces.

Between two people different types of silence are possible. The first in which the unsaid or mulled-over intention glitters and vaults like a tumbler - this is conversational silence; it is slave, messenger and under-study for words. While the other silence, the silence beyond words, is a true silence, because it occurs when words are superfluous, transcended, exhausted...in the soft nest of love, under the mantle of suffocating hate, in the cemetery of past feelings overgrown by weeds and grass, here or there, but beyond words. (The story of these three will soon come to this...)

Finally Ferenc Révay broke the harmonious silence with his loud monotone: Why didn't they give up this whole ridiculous comedy? The winter had been long and hard...exhausting. He would not hurt Susanna Forgách ever again, that was certain...

"You promised this once already."

He would repeat his testimony, gladly and honestly, Ferenc replied.

"Then why not put it in writing?" asked the other. If the intention is really honest, in writing or not, in a safe place, here or there, in the apostle's pocket or the devil's box, is it not all the same? Otherwise a separation must take place tomorrow...

Then Ferenc Révay handed Peter Bakics the paper. But if he had not signed it, how would Peter prove what was on it? With witnesses, replied the other. But this was absurd, Ferenc retorted, for others in the castle would offer evidence against Peter too...

"Not here," Bakics said, "but I could summon them from Vienna and Prague..." He did not finish the sentence (nor did he need to), and as he said it, he himself was paralysed by fear, a surprising and repugnant nervousness lapped around his words...that he could summon witnesses or call for help from that quarter to expose this rotten and scabrous monstrosity which he loathed from the depths of his heart and which, until he had put it well behind him, he wouldn't believe was real. An abyss opened before him too.

Then Ferenc asked, as he played mischievously with the stem of the pen and snapped it in his fingers, why Peter Bakics, given his determination to make out the seriousness of the case, had not mentioned in the list of offences "my impotence"? - he actually used the word.

"That would be difficult to prove...," the other smiled.

Bakics' simple irony revealed nothing Ferenc could not have found out in eye-opening detail from others, yet he almost choked. He could hardly bear to look at his rival, who now added in a serious tone:

"For the time being it is enough."

Ferenc Révay was silent.

Or perhaps he murmured something about it not being as easy as one imagined, and how he must now go out but would soon return.

Ferenc groped his way along the corridor, dragging his leg a little, leaning against the wall until the yellow balloon of the night-burning oil lamp revealed the door.

First he vomited, and then he sat down on the familiar, solid seat of the privy.

He was ill.

But he could still think. He turned over in his mind the probable consequences - both public and private - of divorce; he tried to create order, to weigh things up. Ideas, contradictory feelings whirled, but one thing stood out.

He must keep his wife at any cost.

He would rather kill Susanna Forgách than lose her. This is what he thought to himself.

This would become from now on his single, perverse pleasure, even if the rest of his life was mere shadows.

And as he slowly walked back, he thought yes, here too, just like his father, only clever pretences and playing for time would help him. Take where you like this infantile list, Bakics, take it, as Count Herberstein took the false news of my father's death, and then who will laugh the devil's laugh? Deceitful laughter bubbled inside him.

Mutatis mutandis. Behold, he is fulfilled.

He went in, strode to the table and silently signed with a flourish, *"Idem qui supra Franciscus de Reva manupropria"* - "Signed by Ferenc Révay in his own hand."

His farewell to Peter Bakics was, "You can do what you like with that paper..." (all the rest remained unsaid).

26

The rest of the year passed quietly at Szklabinya.

If Peter Bakics came, and especially if the two of them could escape from the house on the least pretext, Susanna would launch into compulsive explanations to all the world, sighing greatly, that it was her good fortune he was here, he who looked after her, defended her, supported her, sweet cousin, dear brother, her keeper and guardian, her devoted wakeful protector, strong armed and strong shouldered.

Thus she repeatedly and unbidden (of course!), humbled herself, wreathing herself in love-lorn smiles and calf-eyes.

And she repeatedly proclaimed her innocence in that trembling voice of hers (inwardly she almost believed it herself sometimes, but at other times she almost laughed...):

"What is my crime, my guilt, what are my errors, that my wretched fate showers suffering on my back? I don't know. I carry within me the ballast of my purity. I will never descend to simpering piety, not for the world, but I shy from the ugly slander about me, despicable as it is."

She repeated it again and again, but it fell on deaf ears (which was more humiliating than if her interlocutors had answered back or made gestures at her).

So her soul burned, and her looks belied her that all was as it had been before.

Ferenc Révay almost hid from his wife. They ate separately. If he saw her or Peter Bakics, he turned the corner or rushed into his room. He could not bear to meet them; he couldn't bear their faces.

His imagined sight of them was enough, scenes which he could not live without, which became forces in his inner life. Sometimes they inflamed a wild, sensitive suffering, at other times they created a quagmire of humiliation within him (a bacchanalia of self-torture). He forced himself to see their infinitely varied and choreographed love-making; it stifled and disgusted him, yet made him swoon with desire.

It is interesting that their wildest physical frenzies were easier for him to imagine ("their tumblings" - he spoke of them thus contemptuously before others), than more tender gestures or endearments between them. What they said to each other before, during and after - this he could not conceive at all. But his sensual self-torment would not leave him in peace, so he persisted in trying out the possible formulae of their private mysteries - each sentence sounding more false than the next.

Perhaps that was why he studiously avoided them, because he was afraid that the outer reality might confuse the inner. It might upset the inner world of his suffering, his blind man's struggle for balance. Or perhaps he thought his face would give him away?

Or was he more afraid of the real spectacle of those two, because they wore with pride all the lovers' finery his paltry imagination might dress them in, and more...

So he lived in his own castle as if he were in hiding there.

27

While those three struggled, punished by their own personal demons, and looked for a way out, in the other world István Bocskay, a Protestant noble from Tiszántúl and once a fierce Hapsburg supporter, had roused the malcontents (there were enough of them...) in the cause of freedom, and by the end of the year 1604 had marched triumphantly into the city of Debrecen.

Ferenc Révay grew excited. From every visitor he inquired discreetly, "I suppose Bocskay is stirring," or, "I presume Bocskay is on the move again..."; but he did not want to be open with anybody. (A shame that Peter Bakics could not bring him hot, fresh news...)

Ferenc felt a great longing, an envy of the rebels who now turned towards Europe with appeals "to the whole Christian world" for support against Rudolf's lawless and tyrannical rule. The winds of change beat on the swinging doors of his soul. But he didn't know what to do.

Finally he decided - "for the present", he repeated to himself - to give up Szklabinya voluntarily without a fight to Bocskay's forces, that is, he would not stand against those who pressed him, but he would not stand beside them either.

That is, as we say, neither one nor the other.

He wrote to Bocskay, subtly broaching the possibility of a personal meeting. However, he was answered not by the newly appointed Prince of Transylvania himself, but by one of his lieutenants, politely but guardedly. The gist was that a meeting was unnecessary; they would gladly and with honour count Ferenc Révay among their number.

Offended and disappointed, Ferenc hid the letter in the pages of a cookbook, between oxtail soup and pigeon pie. Then he rearranged the books on the shelf so that the ominous brown spine would not stick out (or slip down), thinking at the same time: why be secretive? He smiled with relief. Finally things had been decided for him.

The same day he had written the letter to the Transylvanian prince, Ferenc had also composed one to György Thurzó in which he sought news and asked Thurzó's advice on his family problem.

The truth was that Ferenc had begun to be troubled by the list of offences he had given to Peter Bakics. It seemed unimportant, he kept telling himself, merely incriminating himself to himself; but if it was really unimportant, why did he go on thinking about it?

His words thus involuntarily turned against themselves. The emptier they seemed, dwindling to nothing, the clearer their meaning became, so clear that the implications of his deed, which had taken refuge slumbering, playing dead, now came forward and roughly discarded all disguises... He felt foolish and mistaken where earlier he had just shrugged his shoulders, indeed in his most self-deluding moments he had felt proud.

Things must go on. This rattled in his brain, although he did not know what exactly must go on, but he was certain that they must. So he rummaged in his brain for small strategies and clever steps to write Thurzó an advice-seeking, informative letter about the affair.

How beautifully Ferenc put everything down - winning confidence and trust in my house, assuaging my suspicions and engaging my friendship, awaking sensual desires, flirting, inflaming the whore's blood, gloatingly offering me the leash of adultery (what's this? what's this?), hiding his knife under his cloak, tricking me out of my rights, sullying my pure bed, muddying and trampling underfoot my honour, spitting out orders to me...

The letter was full of knavery and elegance, the venom of suffering, death's poisoned wine, the opium of friendship, deep, disguised kisses, *succubi* and *incubi* and who knows what other mires of iniquity. Private tragedy, private comedy, he poured all this out fluently and sent it off to the Viennese Court.

György Thurzó replied understandably quickly. In truth he was (if only out of a heightened sense of his own delicate and important role) extremely concerned about where his family relations would turn at the next cross-road of our Hungarian Romance.

He opened his letter by strongly advising Ferenc Révay not to "rub shoulders with the armed rebels". Had he heard so soon about the abortive message to Bocskay? (The ways and means of betrayal are unknowable...) In any case Ferenc was surprised by Thurzó's direct statement, which did not accord with his usual courtier's circumlocutions. The letter went on to assert that all waverers must now decide (Did he classify Ferenc as one? It was not clear...). "Remember, we sympathise with the Archduke! Now everything depends on us. On us who stand beside the law and our Emperor. Because if we, the last remaining ones, become singed like stupid moths by this emphemeral fire, all is lost, believe me, all. We will be burnt at the stake..." So Thurzó preached, then concluded with pathetic exaggeration: "Understand that we alone, by our steadfastness, can save those who at this moment triumph in their short-lived victory!"

Of course Ferenc understood and even felt that Thurzó was right; but he felt for the rebels, too. However, he didn't believe blindly in either side, and he felt like a lonely reed whipped between two great winds.

Last (but not least) the writer turned to Ferenc's "family problem", the devil's brew of his private life. First, Thurzó was emphatic that Ferenc must show great tolerance over what had happened. The excesses of the heart are cured by changes of circumstance that allow it to find its way naturally back into a more peaceful channel. They should therefore move to such a place where Susanna ("my mad but beautiful sister") would not be able so freely to wander...

Thurzó judged Holics Castle to be eminently suitable for this, surrounded as it is by wide and deep rivers across which even a fiery, female devil could not leap. Though her confinement might irk her, she would be unable to do anything about it.

Thurzó's solution had one gaping flaw, that a wing of Holics Castle belonged to a branch of Peter Bakics' family... Ferenc was astonished that the far-sighted Thurzó could have overlooked this (a pivotal question of our Hungarian Romance...).

Nevertheless, the following day he received a letter from Holics itself, full of Maria's moans and commands, her seethings and presentiments of evil about her sister's downfall (there are few things of which people talk more freely than a prophecy fulfilled, especially a bad one...). Maria greatly admired Thurzó's cleverness, and seconded his persuasions that Ferenc should go thither.

Peter Révay could not understand what the move would accomplish, but could not argue when gripped in the vice of wisdom. He simply added to Maria's imperatives, that according to "our friend" this would be the best for everyone, "because who knows in this mad world how things will turn out?"

Ferenc also, after initial and natural opposition, perceived the line of argument and changed his mind. Why not accept the offer? Move to Holics, stretch matters to their limit and bring them to a head so that they show themselves in black and white. Perhaps this would help... (The silence of the storm, the storm of silence - in what else can people hope?)

Sometimes he still thought of going to Bocskay and his rebels, because what would History think of those who stayed away, neither exalting in victory nor sharing defeat, and by their silence voting for tyranny? He could join the caper and dance away from the stocks confining and tormenting him, out of his private trap. How simply, indeed, elegantly he could discard it; for is there a more elegant role than the man who chooses freedom? Thus History, that great and gallant lord, would give him more that just a way out, indeed a chance to be reborn.

But he did not dare.

28

As the carriages danced along the rough road to Holics, Susanna too felt that History had saved her, and in her happiness could not praise enough that lavish Maecenas who had intervened to protect her, to indulge her, and now to bring her closer and closer to Peter Bakics.

(In our Hungarian Romance this would be neither the first nor the last of death's dances. Others still rougher would follow in which different characters from antiquity would show themselves, especially Judas, that most singular survivor of the classical - and modern - style...)

Honeyed months of freedom followed.

In the spring North Hungary was all aflame, and those flames wrote on the sky's blue sheet FREEDOM in huge letters. The rhythm of the word throbbed life into castles and hovels, into applauding and celebrating sermons. With the first lilacs and the never-before-seen orange trees budded and flowered this mysterious freedom.

But is there really any such thing as freedom? Is it not merely the ghost of denial and yearning, the glow of childish schemes? Can anything more concrete be assumed for it?

Of course we assume we can distinguish good from evil - even from a distance, the very furthest distance, and no matter what cynical or deceitful indicators there may be that these things are really the same. So too, we humbly declare the supremacy of our freedom, if we finally manage to take possession of it. We stretch out eager hands and lift eyes dewed with tears, then immediately create our own - real or imagined - contradictions (only those who have never possessed it believe otherwise).

István Bocskay now was declared the chosen prince of the whole of Hungary. Half the country danced with joy (the other half quaked with terror...).

"I saw no one whose eyes did not shed tears of joy, as sons rediscovered their long lost belief in their fathers" (Bocskay's court priest).

And Susanna Forgách cried with joy as she stepped through the gate of Holics Castle. And Peter Bakics happily came to stay in his long-disused domain. Windows were joyfully cleaned, door-handles polished, lamps rubbed, curtains washed and ironed, larders filled, chimneys swept.

The castle had three relatively independent parts. Upstairs lived the Peter Révays, Ferenc and Susanna took the ground floor, and Peter Bakics owned a separate wing that lay to one side of the building. After their move the whole variety of life was to be found here: upstairs, faith; downstairs, hope; and beside them, love... Truly everything.

Peter Révay during these burning months could not really stir from Thurzó's side in Vienna. And Maria was again expecting a baby (her husband found only a short visit necessary).

When they arrived, Maria had declared that under no condition was her sister to be allowed near her. From then on, of course, the expectant Maria waited for that very visit, for that moment when an embarrassed serving maid would put her head round the door, whispering she did not know what to do because Mistress Susanna was coming, her full skirts were swishing through the narrow corridor, and soon she would be here...

But it did not happen. To be honest, Susanna had not the least intention of seeking a meeting with Maria.

Soon after, Peter Bakics' older sister Margit moved into the castle. She was to look after Susanna when her brother had to travel.

"I'm certain you'll become great friends!" said Peter Bakics to Susanna, adding that poor Margit had recently been widowed, that she had also had an unlucky love - a secret love that had come to nothing - and that his sister could draw beautifully. Sometimes instead of signing her letters she drew small pictures, landscapes, animals or flowers.

Margit had the same black hair and burning looks as her brother. Her eyes, too, shone with wild daring. She was adept in masks, fashions, amusements; and she could make a festival out of a weekday with dancing, wine and music. "Peter, see how happy we are!" - she would say, as free from care and formality as if she and Susanna were old friends. The better to amuse themselves, Margit had two men's suits made - for her a bright red one and a garnet one for Susanna.

Ferenc Révay held their friendship in profound contempt, as anyone would who stands to lose.

One afternoon Margit and Susanna set out to the neighbouring village, dressed in their men's garb (how indispensable it was to the sweet aura and illusion of freedom!). In their breeches and their frock-coats made from the light, stiff brocade, with their hair twisted up and hidden under their hats, they rode splendidly through fields and meadows.

Margit's fleet figure in her red suit blazed stridently and provocatively: the transparent red of poppies, the thick, burning red of flowing blood, the red of clowns and showmen, fresh paint, the rich red dignity of cardinals. Susanna in her garnet clothes was a deeper distillation of Margit's fire, like the flesh and juice of pomegranates.

Side by side they trotted into the village. There they passed the time dancing, then hired minstrels and actors for a procession along the river bank. In front went a gypsy violinist, behind him the two friends. Margit directed all, and Susanna followed unquestioning, yearning for the distant Peter Bakics.

They left their horses tied up on the edge of the village. Ferenc Révay damned and cursed them, as if these patient, expectant animals embodied and made manifest the disaster falling on him from the thundering sky.

That summer more than the air boiled between the thick walls of Holics. Lust singed the rotten beams and heated the mouldy chambers; desire for freedom blew and rained through long-uninhabited halls; profligate, illegitimate loves multiplied... (Children were also born, to what sort of future, poor things, who knows?) In Holics, almost everyone rendered homage to love's religion! (Later Ferenc Révay dismissed without pay all those couples who were not married.)

On summer nights they passed through the corridors on tiptoe, even when it was unnecessary because Ferenc Révay had fallen into a drunken dream (to which Margit Bakics' sleeping draughts had charitably contributed); Maria lay helplessly in confinement. Rustling skirts, the music of creaking floors under boot heels, whispered words. The candles in their hands were like August lightning or falling stars when somebody stepped out of - or through - a door or branched off at a corner... During the day they wrote burning notes, under cover of dawn they stole from one floor to another.

"All change" - thus it was later described. Black Masses were rumoured, pacts with corrupt souls from the other side of the moon, flitting, so it was said, between Holics' strong walls, or in the meadow all joining hands, where unholy acquaintances were made in the centre of the circle - so the gossips made out the choreography. Everyone fell in love at first sight, feelings went naked...and long after, the people in the area called this period "the time of the great landslide", mixing it up so thoroughly, confusing lovers' stories and historical events until it was impossible to know what this title referred to: whether to the time when Bocskay's army marched to Kosice, or when István the Scribe appeared in the castle courtyard after a dawn bath with the fragile, naked Barbara on his back, her legs dangling. It was chiefly these dawn or nighttime swims that gave rise to the juiciest legends...

They raced to the nearby river where the water was silky and gentle. In its dark mirror lay wan strips of moonlight, its subtle, wavering rays created islands which were scattered by the swimmers. Only a splash indicated their presence. While others might laugh and shriek, Peter and Susanna grew sleek in the water, like wild ducks.

When they came out, shivering and cold, the air was chilly. Each rubbed down the other with rough linen. As Peter Bakics wrapped up Susanna to dry her, they became so warm, their bodies seemed to burn. With their skin tingling, they found their clothes light and chill as if their bodies had left no trace in them. They left refreshed and went directly to Peter's bed.

Strange how deceiving was this great burning sensation on the skin; for when they embraced, each felt the other's body was cold. As Susanna wound her bare arms around him, Peter Bakics felt her thighs colder than the first snows. Susanna, too, felt the man's stomach, as it pressed and caressed her, was cold.

Sometimes the question of the future intruded, was revived between them, as she sat up in bed, or he leant down over her, contemplating her softly and uncertainly: what will happen to us? ("What will happen to us, darling?") Then it was always in a compelling, resolute, and at the same time alleviating, aggravating (fatal) and of course fanciful manner that the man would say, "I love you", as if these three words alone could solve everything - the protective shade of their love, its gilded nest - as if they could encompass and answer the chaos reigning in their lives.

As a boy Peter Bakics had often bathed with the Révay brothers - so he told Susanna one day. Orphaned young, he had moved in with them for a time; a lower-ranking relation moving in with the higher, yet he received a warm welcome, though not long after, the Révays' father died.

It seemed that this unexpected return to Holics had revived many memories.

How they had sat on the grass, their bare backs burning in the sun, their legs covered in bruises. When they could no longer bear the heat, being too lazy to swim, they would sprinkle handfuls of water over each other. Often it was just the two of them, for Peter Révay had to study in the coldest corner of a chill chamber.

Ferenc Révay once found a knife in the water-washed sand. (Why is it so pleasant? Just one movement, and all the dirt and mud disappear...just a movement of the hand - perhaps that is why we love to grub about in the mud by the water.) It was a fine knife, double-edged, with a narrow blade and a strong hilt, probably made of silver, and immediately Ferenc had given it to Peter. It suits you better, Ferenc had said, without any reluctance or self-pity. After soberly twirling it in his hand he offered it to Peter, shrugging off all protestations. However, Peter, in trying it out, had aimed and thrown it at a narrow-trunked tree in the woods... They searched for it among the knee-high burdocks, but it never reappeared.

Susanna did not like it when Peter Bakics talked about this shared childhood. Since Ferenc had signed his testimony, she had thought of him quite impersonally as a strategist, a planner of measures and counter-measures, the X factor in her life. She was afraid that she would step on the knife which her husband had found and lose her lover in the grass.

29

A life of paradoxes, far from the stars and close to the fire all at once.

As the scent of scandal wafted under the castle-dwellers' noses (since the "nuptial days" in any case), everybody rushed to join in, throwing their lot in with one side or the other.

The most resourceful ones (the opportunists) were the fastest to profit from declaring themselves. It took no education to realise that "Fortune favours the brave", that is, those who smell out the turning points of an unclear situation and take quick action. (These people were following the same intuition as the highly educated György Thurzó when he supported the fantasies of Archduke Mátyás against Mad Rudolf. In these instances learning counts about as much as a splash of French perfume on an unwashed body.)

There were plenty of others who remained uncertain, who did not want to take unnecessary risks by prematurely speaking their minds. They assumed a "wait and see" position...in the *let's see how things turn out* tradition.

The most biased and partial was Ferenc Révay's steward, who represented his master's interests strictly and loudly as if they were his own. He even took a reproving tone with his master, supposedly even shouting at him.

There were those who favoured the tale-bearing, muck-raking jackdaw's role, while others did no more than jingle the soothing change in their pockets. And for the role of the grubby secret advisor, who else could be more suitable than the priest?

Zealous informers told Maria the news; and the midwives and nurses feared her temperature would rise, her mouth run dry and her appetite disappear.

Disguise and pretence also, of course, played their part for the lovers. Susanna's serving women were enlisted on the side of love, as were Peter Bakics' men. There was Bakics' most intimate friend and follower, Gábor Somogyi, a sauntering, ragged nobleman; then there was his page, Daniel Viktorin, who moreover was in love with Susanna. If he met her, while giving or taking messages, he blushed...and inwardly? Inwardly wilder than wild dreams were the stuff of Daniel's love; yet he fulfilled his delicate and dangerous tasks quite conscientiously.

In the repertory of roles there were naturally a range of extras: smiling and grinning hyenas, sneaking kibitzers mad for revenge, amateur Lucifers, silent partners and so on and so on.

A thirst for gossip, axes to grind, *parlez l'amour c'est faire l'amour*...everything which is usual at such times.

30

After she had given birth, Maria in her solitude relented towards her sister.

She lay there in her sick-room, a lump in her throat, weak, ill and lonely. This despite the fact that midwives and nurses whispered and bustled constantly about her, around the duck-beaked jugs, the rounded wash bowls, disinfectants, boiled linen and spare blankets. The newborn's cradle was beside her bed - she was only strong enough sometimes to raise her thin white arms from under the covers, grip the rim of the cradle and rock the crying child. The busy women about her arranged the sheets beneath her; they covered their palms with strong concoctions as they lifted her; if her fever rose they wrapped her in wet garments so that her body shivered. Only the sight of the child, the chance to stroke the tiny face peering from under the huge bonnet, or carefully to touch the tiny hands gave Maria joy and spiritual repose.

On one of these solitary afternoons when the nurses had closed the curtains so that she would sleep, but she couldn't, she thought... This allowed her gentler emotions to gain ground over her anger, and something changed within her. She would gladly forgive her sister, and perhaps Susanna could gently forget the hurts held since childhood (adulthood). Maria felt she could be a sympathetic listener and even confederate in secrets, if Susanna would come to her, take her hand, look into her eyes, lead her into unknown territories, where the afternoons were melodious, but where people could also find snakes or scorpions in their shoes.

She decided that her sister should sleep beside her and then they could speak till dawn, make up for the neglect in their girlhood. Maria chose a pearl to give her and an ornament for her hair. Then she thought she would ask Susanna to comb her hair, which had become so tangled in labour that no one had been able to brush it out since.

She imagined her sister rocking the baby as if it were her own, just as she, Maria, would rock her sister's baby if she ever had one. Now Maria looked lovingly at everything as if through her sister's eyes, and saw how much Susanna missed affection, especially from her husband... For Ferenc had met Susanna when she was already dissembling her feelings like a hedgehog, as she had done throughout her childhood.

Maria then sent a message to her sister asking her lovingly to visit. Hunger and thirst could not have been more consuming than Maria's longing - there was no escaping it.

But Susanna did not go up to her. Did she not notice the tone of the message, its burning strangeness? She was now completely preoccupied with her lover.

Maria waited in ever-greater disappointment, and then on the third day of this fruitless wait there was a change. She got up, retching with pain, and supported by two old women set off down the stairs to the ground floor.

Moving with tiny, shuffling steps, half-way there Maria started to feel giddy, but she didn't give up her intention to tell her sister (with the two old women like black crows on either side), "Do you know what will await you if you don't come to your senses soon?

"This Peter Bakics... (a pouting smile, a supercilious wave of the hand as if a throne-room span, a length of mirrored floor and a dozen crested halberds separated them), he will leave you... You are neither the first nor the last, believe me (here one of the old crows interjected 'that is certain!'). If, however, you do not believe us," Maria with a grandiose gesture included the old women in her chorus, "ask his sister, your friend, she can tell you about several of them; your dear Margit, who poisoned that poor good Menyhert Balassa" (and one of the women - the same one or another? no matter - echoed, open-mouthed, "True!" thus fulfilling her role).

Maria continued, "If he does not abandon you now, then I prophesy that you will become a stone around his neck, do you want that? Or perhaps you will ruin him, too? Such a stinking scandal will only discredit him before others and before God! Have you not thought of that?"

She talked on and on, no cliché was left out: banging heads against brick walls, pride going before a fall, iniquities and commandments; torments and damnation, dried-up vessels, crocodile tears, pretences, fasts of repentance, frolicking, schemes, even trampling on the mount of Venus, drowning sorrows in drink, in the catacombs, in curses and hells.

During her speech Maria's face became increasingly pale, her forehead pearled with sweat. It seemed that she could hardly bear her afflictions. But all words were in vain, even her most select ones.

Susanna just sat smiling, her hands limp in her lap, and

only when her sister's speech had run out, did she speak for the first time.

She said that she and Peter Bakics loved each other with their whole, pure hearts... Susanna said she forgave Maria for not understanding; perhaps she did not know what this meant.

Maria stood up. "If that is what you wish."

The old women flew after her like black dust clouds.

31

A wild and desperate alliance was forged between Ferenc Révay and Maria Forgách.

But - perhaps precisely because of it - their relationship chiefly consisted of castigating the sinners. Maria soon recognised that her encouragement to Ferenc Révay to take stronger measures against the lovers was useless. Ferenc covered himself in silence; he stood beside Maria's sick-bed nodding, but nothing more. His only interest was to blame them.

He did not speak much about his wife or if he did, he mentioned her only with general or clipped subjectivity - as if her name held all the infectious discharge of sin, all the monstrousness of outraged feeling. He simply could not bear to say Susanna's name aloud and superstitiously shrank from it. (Only the trial records and charges forced him, later, to break this silence; the alienation and objectivity of the legal necessities of a divorce - why is it precisely the phobias and spasms which are never got rid of, even at the final bankruptcy sale?) But he abused Peter Bakics by name and for hours, hatred foaming within him. Maria sought to defend Peter Bakics, to convince Ferenc that it was not the man who was chiefly at fault, "Believe me, that unlucky Peter cannot do anything, he's driven mad, just as that poor musician was...and like the musician, Bakics should be sent away."

But when Maria roused herself spluttering and gripping the pillow, calling her sister "whore", "wretch", and "filth" (why catalogue the choking ivy of hate?), Ferenc Révay closed himself off, hid behind an impenetrable mask (since the move to Holics this habit had grown worse). Indeed, sometimes he even shuddered when Maria drew the longbow to slander her sister.

So that despite their wild and desperate alliance, they could not really come to an understanding.

32

Ferenc was upstairs with Maria when Peter Bakics celebrated his birthday. Bakics had asked many people from the surrounding manors, villages and towns; one after another the carriages filled with happy, well-dressed people drew up (the fight for freedom was hundreds of kilometres away, so that it was possible to celebrate in peace...).

Ferenc Révay watched them from the tower room above and was filled with satisfaction that at last he, he alone, controlled events.

And indeed the guests talked long afterwards of the pleasures and spectacles to be had in that garden. Not only because the long wooden trestles in the shadows of the trees groaned with huge platters and tall jugs; not only because the garden trees and bushes were strung with colourful ribbons of red, and with orange, lilac and

green lamps of a richness not before seen; not only
because ripe fruit in abundance was at hand; not only
because before dusk a heavy summer shower streamed
onto their heads, beating on the benches, tables and
barrels, while they waited for it to end under spreads and
covers, then danced barefoot in the close, soft warmth,
on the wet grass, re-lighting the hastily gathered up oil
lamps; not only because with frenzied measures they went
on dancing, while above, in the blue-grey hills, the sun
tumbled among the lilac and red ripples of the sky;
because they danced into the night without ceasing, and
one musician (supposedly) fell dead from exhaustion, still
clutching his instrument; not only because Peter Bakics
and Susanna Forgách openly went hand in hand as
lovers; not only because the strong light of the lamps
varnished the leaves with orange, scarlet and lilac light,
leaving the trunks of the trees in pleasing darkness.

It was chiefly memorable because, in that garden of
delights, Ferenc Révay tried to poison Peter Bakics.

Just as they toasted the host with glass in hand, and
Susanna laid out the presents (for weeks she had been
occupied sewing shirts and other garments for her man),
a small boy proffered Peter Bakics a tiny rolled up note.
A holy wafer from the Pope's hand could not have been
lighter and whiter. At first Peter believed it to be a
celebratory verse...

You shall perish.

That was all. No signature. Of course everyone was
immediately curious to know, what is it? What is it? Peter
Bakics read it out clearly and loudly and asked (rituals,
rituals), who wrote it?

For want of an answer the small boy was brought
forward, but could say only that it had been pressed into
his hand behind a tree.

"Let's forget it," said Peter Bakics. Only Susanna
trembled, and when the man raised his glass high, she,

her presentiments correctly guiding her, whispered to him, "Don't drink it! don't drink it!"

The ill-effects followed after about ten minutes. Strong giddiness, shivering and weakness which were impossible to master, as if he were hauling around his own body: faces blurred, things disintegrated in his sight, azure streams of sweat ran into his eyes, his mouth; his hands went cold as sepulchres, completely numb; only after they laid him down on his cloak under a tree, under Susanna's direction, with her tears, kisses, her handkerchief on his forehead, did he vomit convulsively.

Then he slept and at last breathed steadily and peacefully.

Ferenc Révay up in the tower saw the developments with mixed feelings. He watched his rival's agony (he believed) with satisfaction, and his resuscitation with relief.

The truth was that not long before the day of the garden party the resourceful Kutsera had come to Ferenc Révay, saying that he had heard something really interesting from some trustworthy person in Bakics' employ, that Susanna and her friend Margit had decided "to do away with the Master by poison, while celebrating Peter Bakics' birthday, so he would no longer vex them..."

Where did she get the poison? This was of primary interest to Ferenc Révay. In a strange way the news did not appear to shake him - as if he had expected something like this. Kutsera had not really wanted to take revenge on anyone, but when Ferenc Révay asked him exactly when this damned birthday would come, then he, Kutsera (as he later confessed), understood his meaning and the following day gave his Master a small bag. Ferenc Révay first tried his dog with the poison, the greyhound he loathed because it always fawned on Peter Bakics.

But then his accomplice Kutsera (as he later declared) pondered the thing, that whatever perfidious, hawkish crimes those two would sink to - he would rather trust God's justice to punish them. Thus the next day he changed the contents of the bag for a harmless emetic, and, knowing that it was harmless, he decided to empty the powder into Peter Bakics' glass at an opportune moment. He thought perhaps it would not be so bad, when the Master's wrath subsided, he would probably be terrified of what he had intended to do and would not try it again (the servant's testimony revealed long experience of human nature). But he swore he had nothing to do with and knew nothing about the threatening note.

The note was followed, however, by others addressed to Susanna. Every night they were slipped into her room in the form of pellets under the door. (Why were they kneaded together so that one had to keep unfolding them, it was incomprehensible!) The anonymous writer varied his verbs, but not his meaning: "You shall perish," "You shall die," "You shall rot." Although the linguistic possibilities were not endless, the store of feelings was clearly bottomless, and when his stock of words ran out, the letter-writer simply started from the beginning, a threat for each day.

Who wrote these never came to light.

Ferenc Révay himself also started to show around similar notes he purported to have received. This was strange. But Peter Bakics told Susanna not to concern herself, he was sure that Ferenc wrote the notes to himself to confuse the already tangled threads.

At that time Ferenc also began to tell the world that he knew his wife, with the help of "that slut" (Margit Bakics), wanted to poison him... He gladly and expansively told this story, sometimes forgetting that he had told it only an hour before. But he did not personally try any poisoning again.

33

See how this came about:

Margit and Susanna had gone into the woods, down to the pebbly stream where salamanders rested on the stones, those strange beings with their yellow-smudged, black-varnished elegance and their visibly heavy heart-beats in their breasts. From the stream bank they wanted to gather grass stems which Margit would mark - one stem for each of them - and hang from a high rafter: whoever's stem dried first would die soonest... Properly they should have been collected from under a gallows, but as there were none nearby, the stream bank would have to do.

The air was close and sultry. The leaves were still, brimming grey clouds passed overhead. Margit shrugged her shoulders and said it was not important; the rain would be warm, and if it rained, they could bathe in it. But only a few drops fell on their fingers and noses.

Margit Bakics moved about, completely at ease, with a mysterious smile on her lips. She spoke of the wild boar in its hiding places, of the hiding places of the red and roe deer, of how during a walk in the woods once, a red deer had followed her several miles. She did not know what it wanted from her, but it would not stir from her side. Then she talked of how glad she was that her brother Peter was at last in love - this word she knew how to say as if all the rapture and sadness, force and weakness, sin and absolution of the world were con-densed there, and as she said it her voice changed, becoming a little reluctant, tremulous and tearful.

"I hope," she clasped Susanna's hand, "that you really will love Peter..." Her tone was needlessly pressing on this point (was she unaware that some walk hand in hand not merely to flick the dust from each others' clothes?). And then, without waiting for Susanna's reply, she started to explain that she knew the meaning of love because...while her husband yet lived ("God rest him, poor thing!" - she crossed herself, but the gesture was so perfunctory it was rather as if she drew an undulating line in the air. Impossible to know for certain what this appendix - "poor thing" - referred to, whether to the deceased in life or death), she had been in love. The person was old enough to be her father, but it hadn't mattered at all, truly. She became disillusioned, however, because their great love had come to nothing...

"Why?" asked Susanna. But Margit Bakics suddenly withdrew, shrugging her shoulders phlegmatically. One felt that this seemingly instinctive gesture hid careful and quickly spinning thoughts.

"Because it did not..." she replied. After that it was impossible to get another word out of her. It seemed that between the sparkling surface of Margit's personality and its unreachable core there was no connection, and she had no ambition to make one.

Susanna could not pin-point the reason, but from the day of that walk in the woods with Margit, she could no longer feel the same unambiguous affection toward her friend.

Towards home they were caught in the rain and had to run, Susanna gripping the grass stems, so as not to lose them. When they were just at the gate, they came face to face with Ferenc. The women's light summer garments clung to their bodies and water streamed from their hair.

Usually he would have turned to avoid them.

"Have you gone mad?" he asked Susanna. He seemed not to notice Margit.

The women did not deign to reply. After a few steps they stopped and turned around. Margit asked in a loud voice, "Where do you think that fool is going in the rain?"

So now they had called him "fool" for the first time within earshot, and they watched his helpless writhings with delight.

This came to pass only a week before the birthday feast.

34

Maria was horrified by the poisoning. She distanced herself (far, far) from any real forms of destruction; she shrank in dread from such things. But she had watched Ferenc's face carefully as he had stood by the window on that day. She too had leaned out and watched the throng around the body on the ground (dropped masks, whirling clothes and disguises, costumes in crazy patterns, hooded jerkins, zig-zagged robes) and had asked, who was it?

"Peter Bakics," Ferenc had replied. He usually decked out any mention of that name with intricate curses, kitchen swear-words and exorcising imprecations. Now Maria saw such a display of unconcern and indifference that the man betrayed himself.

In agitation Maria wrote to her husband, telling him to hurry home. But Peter Révay could not come: he was awaiting the return of Thurzó who, along with the bishop Ferenc Forgách, had initiated peace talks with the rebels on the Emperor's behalf. "If he comes we shall be wiser..." It was impossible to know what Peter was referring to: the remedy for private misery or public calamity? (Perhaps both...)

Then Maria sent Thurzó himself a letter; his reply was a gift basket of game birds and a few crumple-faced pomegranates. But when Maria undid the basket, she started to cry. A stench came up from the dead pheasants, which had decomposed on the journey. Maria cried hysterically, as if these dead-eyed messengers were birds of ill omen, prophetic of impending doom.

She wrote again to Thurzó, reproaching him for the first time in her life. Saying that a snake lay on their breasts and that disgrace had fallen upon the family.

Thurzó asked her patience, but he could not come yet.

In the calm after the storm, he must wash the floor, cover up the traces and strew with ashes the subsiding flames of rebellion.

How the Wind Changes
(History Lesson No.4)

Immediately on his arrival on Polish soil, István
Illésházy began to write letters. Not for a moment
did he leave in peace his pursuers or forget his
friends. He nurtured and sustained old connections.
He could now disgorge his formerly restrained
emotions, spew out his venom from the distance of
exile. But he took care never to break the narrow
thread that might guide his return.

He castigated everyone who played a role in his
illegal trial. Here is the letter he sent to Istvánffy,
the President of the Court, "Can the country bear it,
if its rules are broken, its judgements corrupted by
favouritism or hate?" He wrote similarly to all the
judges. But never once did he question the rightness
of Hapsburg Imperial claims to rule Hungary. It
seems he had taken his tattered bundle of loyalty
with him over the border.

Or was it a question of political expediency? His
family were still in Hungary, and his property still
remained to be confiscated.

When the time came, however, the executors
overlooked nothing: vases, books, horses. They
confiscated his wife's clothes, but this was not
enough. The wardrobes of all the noblewomen in
the castle were also crammed into sacks and carted
away, leaving only what they wore on their backs.
And as a number of the young girls were preparing
to marry at the time, their dower chests were

plundered. Black footprints were left in the snow, and sobbing and wailing was heard in the castle. The girls, in their remaining threads, immediately petitioned the Archduke for mercy (and postponed their weddings).

But Archduke Mátyás did not wish to confront the Prague Treasury over a minor matter of missing stockings and lacy underwear. So, as the girls with their disappointed grooms stood in semi-circle at the palace entrance, weeping reproachful tears, he made use of a secret exit...

Gloat as he might over his brother's error, the Archduke did not try for a moment to turn the scandal to his advantage. Not a single petitioner did he summon to choose her wedding garments from among his treasures, from the Imperial stores in half-lit rooms where he and that lovely supplicant might have rummaged about, hand touching fumbling hand...

No, he did not do it. For him the whole piece of incomprehensible fanaticism was unpleasant enough, but he was now more concerned to exploit the opportunities created by new winds blowing over Hungary... In this he followed a similar tactic to Illésházy - one helping the other, need we say more?

When the first breath of rebellion reached Illésházy's sensitive and subtle ears, it immediately dawned on him that his situation as exile and survivor was tailor-made for the role of mediator. Despite his disadvantaged position, he would be the first to try to bring both sides together (there might be advantage in it if the wind changed!).

So Illésházy carefully preserved his loyalty (or the illusion of it), not reneging even when the rebel Bocskay pressed him in these terms, "I see your Lordship not only as my friend, but as my father..."

So wrote Hungary's newly elected prince to the refugee in his miserable exile... Is it any accident that nowadays - whatever allowances one might make for the rhetorical styles of different ages - no one would think to call upon their fathers with such confidence and honour? No, it is not an accident...

It was after the Archduke had received (by the most secret and confidential channels) Bocskay's letter from Illésházy (Judases, Judases as far as the eye can see...) and had been warned not to ignore the enormity of the danger, that he hurriedly submitted to the Emperor the first appeal for mercy in Illésházy's case.

Rudolf denied it directly.

The revolt spread.

The Archduke tried again. It was no easy thing: there were enemies of his around the Emperor, plenty of them. For example, the fanatical Szuhay again engaged himself to persuade Rudolf that they must press for extradition of the criminal Illésházy, because otherwise...(the old arguments and examples were again laid out).

On this mission Szuhay personally went to Rudolf in his gallery, where he found the Emperor contemplating a picture on an easel, undeniably one by Master Arcimboldo...a mad painter for a mad Emperor, how suitable!

The canvas, "the calumny" (as Szuhay called it to himself) was of a man's head. The hair was red tongues of flame and suggestive antlers; the cheeks, two purple onions topped by a hairy wart; the neck was a golden goblet; the ears were poppies; the shirt-collar was scalloped from white radish flowers; the frill was a carrot, its green top just visible; the eyes were glass balls; the mouth from the swollen, chapped flesh of a mushroom...

Rudolf, bewitched, was gazing at the picture as Szuhay started to speak. But his voice died away when the Emperor did not look at him. As Szuhay stepped nearer to start again, Rudolf almost smacked him with his rings, his fat hand roughly gesturing for him to remove himself so as not to block the view of the picture. Then Szuhay from a safe distance began again, that if they set the criminal free, in future it would be difficult to find councillors who would undertake to serve so loyally in such cases...

"Perhaps if I became a rebel, then I would be granted grace," complained Illésházy to the Archduke, after the Emperor had refused the Archduke's second appeal for mercy. (Familiar, is it not? Only a minute ago a similar argument issued from Szuhay's mouth...indignation disguised as loyalty and discreet betrayal from both prosecutor and accused... However lamentable history may be, one cannot deny the mean and unchanging logic of things.) Just as news arrived in Prague that Illésházy in his final despair had joined the rebels, with much huffing and grumbling, his rehabilitation began!

The Prague Court officially stated that the trial had been "impetuous and incorrect". Which also meant that the officials who had earlier screamed and squawked for Illésházy's head were now pointing fingers at one another in a game of "pin the tail on the donkey". That is, not at each other, as one German at another, but at the Hungarian participants in the trial.

The Hungarians. Including Szuhay. (In History's grand depository, under the title "the Moor did it", many similar episodes can be found.)

Illésházy's defection was received by Bocskay with joy and celebration. He immediately declared

Illésházy his captain-in-chief and gave him Trencsén Castle. Illésházy now concentrated on drawing up peace negotiations - with his Prince putting the finishing touches to their demands for religious freedom and civil government. On the question of Transylvania, the political dilemma of the age, each man embodied a different side of the problem.

Illésházy wanted a united Hungary, if it could not be done in any other way, then under the Hapsburg crown. Bocskay wanted an independent Transylvania, as foundation for the rest of Hungary, until the whole country was free.

György Thurzó was sent to negotiate and bargain for the Hapsburgs on behalf of the Emperor (that is, on behalf of his younger brother).

Thurzó and Illésházy (who was the turncoat now? no matter), finding common interests and aims, did not touch on the past, indeed they studiously avoided it (a neutral "it should not have been allowed" and "there was no other choice" perhaps came up when they appeared at the second meeting). Together they sat by the bed of the now dying Bocskay, placing fresh pillows, filling his water glass, rearranging the blankets on his legs, taking his pulse instead of the doctors, while his weakening will, his fading voice grew exhausted and fainter against their united and harmonious refrain. One by one they whittled away at the conditions for peace, recomposed them, toned them down, filled them with loopholes that conformed with Archduke Mátyás' interests.

The peace treaty was a personal victory for the Archduke (finders-keepers), and there were vanquished on all sides. Twenty thousand Hungarians (here's a change!) marched into Prague, and the Imperial brother with his own gloved hands closed the barred gates of his apartments. Mátyás took up quarters in Hradzsin Castle, mad Rudolf was forced to abdicate first the Hungarian, and then the Czech crown in favour of his brother. ("Cain and Cain" and "my enemy's enemy...," history has many such archetypes.)

So the Imperial brothers lived side by side for five months under the same roof, but did not meet once. Rudolf hid in his inner chambers, with curtains on the doors and windows and wax in his ears so he would not have to hear the impolite acclamations of the king-makers outside. He cowered in his airless room with his horoscopes, his flasks and his favourite lackey (a mere decorative *parvenu*), and would not even venture out into the palace garden for a little air...

The angel of death might have spread a shroud, a *tabula rasa* before us.

If it was so simple.

But the angel of death lurked mischievously just offstage.

On his return from exile Illésházy was received in Vienna with hurried apologies and expressions of thanks...

He got back everything: each silver spoon was counted one by one into his palm; and on the day of Archduke Mátyás' coronation as King of Hungary, he was chosen by his fellow nobles (the day dawned, everybody came...deceptive moment) as the Palatine of Hapsburg-Hungary.

And so he was - for the remaining half year of his life.

The freedom, the praises and honour that fell into his lap, the plentiful compensation - perhaps he saw clearly, too clearly, the motives, heres and nows, pros and cons - or perhaps it was the sticky chain of

betrayal which fettered his feelings of joy? Not that
he was displeased by the frenzied, almost universal
sympathy that flowed toward him from all quarters,
but he felt somewhat ill at ease cast as a symbol...

"I'm tired," he said at the time, "I am exhausted."
Thus he explained to himself his strange indifference. He thought of his heart trouble and his
gastric complaints... (Dances of death, playing Judas,
exiles and rehabilitation - none of these do the heart
any good...it is well known.)

The mourners accompanied his last journey with
glad memories and great pomp (and unsaid
thoughts). On his tombstone (in the sacristy of Bazin
church) was sculpted a proud man of most stately
bearing; in one hand he holds a sceptre, but with
such womanly and ethereal elegance, his hand raised
and tilted back (as Cyprian Virgil Basirius once held
the virginals), while with his other hand he clasps his
helmet in his fingertips. He stands straight-necked,
straight-backed, yet with graceful lightness. And did
the sculptor intend something by the way he carved
his look? While the stony head fronts the spectator
face to face, the eyeholes, with their pupils sliding
toward the corners, are ever on the watch for
someone else.

35

György Thurzó was in high spirits when at last he arrived at Holics, accompanied by Peter Révay. It was entirely understandable. He had seen the fulfilment of the age, the ripening of the rare fruit of bitterness, intrigue and struggle. (Rotten or not, who thinks about these things at such a time?) Why should he conceal his gladness, just because private tragedy or comedy had broken out in the family for the umpteenth time? From his stork's-eye view of public victories and future plans, the personal was easily overlooked. Now that he had satisfactorily brought the great dance to a stately halt, must he gape yokel-like at the tuneless solos of the heart? That was how György Thurzó felt on the day of his arrival.

He had consented to spend the night in the bosom of his dear family, if everybody without exception would be there around him ("I trust that things have not degenerated among you so much into hatred that we cannot sit together at one table...").

Peter Bakics and Susanna Forgách gladly went up to meet him, with special pleasure because they culled from the invitation a faint acceptance of their situation.

Somebody went down to Ferenc Révay to convey the message to him too. He was grateful, but he was not hungry. Not today.

Thurzó shook his head. But really everybody was relieved, the evening started in unusual peace. It seemed as if Thurzó's presence alleviated their raging tensions, as if he had opened around them another, airier and greater space. They could almost breathe freely in this illusory era of peace opened by his presence.

Although the Forgách sisters did not really speak to each other, relations seemed to thaw as Susanna rocked the cradle and talked to the baby, with Peter Bakics crouching beside it. Maria went towards them. (Seizing the opportunity? Or anxiety that the baby might be corrupted? No matter.) A tiny rash had appeared on the small forehead; and Maria, in consideration of their kinship, asked their views on the possible cause.

Although Susanna looked carefully, there was really nothing on the baby's forehead.

György Thurzó ate with gusto and told stories. There was the famous one about Illésházy after he had gone over to Bocskay's camp, how he spent a sleepless night in his tent, shivering to hear nearby the damned, prophetic shrieking of a wretched dervish. Perhaps it was then that Illésházy decided finally to go home...

Thurzó liked this seemingly insignificant story so much that during his stay at Holics he told it many times - it was impossible to know whether he forgot that he had told it already, or whether he just loved hearing it again and again... The incongruity of Illésházy and the howling dervish in the wilderness seemed to Thurzó to sum up the principle of and the key to his own political beliefs. His understanding of the world, his justification for being, were all contained in this anecdote, like a picture incised on a medal.

Otherwise he hardly spoke about public affairs. At one moment he stood up at the supper table and raised his glass - "To Our King Mátyás the Second" - with such naturalness, as if a small army were not just then stationed outside Rudolf's chambers. Though they plagued him with questions about the putsch, he said only that he was now extraordinarily optimistic about the country's affairs, adding, "Believe me, many things will change now."

Meanwhile, the beaming Peter Révay picked up the bundle of swaddling with which Maria presented him and waited for the baby to smile back at him. After Thurzó had called the little girl "my lad" for the second time, Maria had to correct him. Thurzó then appeasingly kissed the thin hand of his "loving sister" and excused himself by reference to his preoccupation with the country's problems; he promised the little one a velvet robe by way of making amends, and for a moment took the bundle from its father's hands. The baby started to cry, the Imperial councillor tried cooing at her, which made the little girl cry harder. She only calmed down when Peter Bakics took her into his arms and sang to her...

Peter Bakics, like Thurzó, had a great bushy beard; but - well, well - the dogs fawned on him and the children smiled at him...

Maria entreated their distinguished relative to stay the night with them, but he declared he would quarter with Bakics because he would be less of a burden to a late-night bachelor. Putting his arm round Peter Bakics' shoulders as he said this last word, Thurzó surprised the Révays. With them he had never been so intimate.

During the evening they again sent for Ferenc, but his room was unlit. Perhaps he had gone out, no one knew where.

He was lying miserably in the darkness, however.

He was waiting for the trap of his own making to close around him. They would either take his wife away from him, forcing him with bowed head to accept defeat, or if he defended himself, then his secret would out and his shame would be cast before the country and the world... A divorce in these uncertain times would be a disaster in every respect.

Yet when Thurzó had summoned him saying, "Come, travel with me to Vienna," where his presence - even on a lightning visit - would be most helpful if only to get his say in first, Ferenc had nodded, but inwardly said no. The sinners must not be left to themselves.

Other things, like the fishing scheduled for the next day in Thurzó's honour, only added to his misery.

For some time now it had been contrived that the three parties to the scandal avoided appearing together before outsiders. Ferenc shunned all curious stares and mocking or pitiful glances of the shop-window variety. How should he behave in this company? With ostentatious and defiant silence? Or should he be provoking and argumentative? Or make light small talk as if nothing had happened? Thurzó's watchful and mediating presence would only aggravate matters.

He had thus decided to stay at home - let them squirm, all of them! Leave Thurzó to see how degenerate things had become. He was filled with almost sensual feelings, near satisfaction, as he imagined the forced and tense voices upstairs this evening, caused by his absence, his trick of absenting himself (*his cold empty place* - but of course Ferenc really considered that his absence was a burning issue...).

The alcohol he had drunk in quantity finally forced him into a heavy sleep.

36

The nearer the boats went towards each other, the further apart they got. As if following a secret dance, they drifted beautifully in circles on the lake, which by its deep blue heralded the approaching autumn. (No one showed the least interest in fishing, only if the fish rose to their nets...)

Their boat, as if blown by the wind or bowled on the glassy water, drifted delicately further and further away until it came to rest where ripe burrs and the brown maces of reeds and bulrushes were entangled. In the veiled silence, the plashing of oars and the others' voices reached them only in snatches, in drawled or disjointed outbursts.

"I want to live with you," said Susanna. Peter Bakics by way of an answer, lifted, in perfect relaxation, her skirt, which was only a shade darker than the lake itself. He kneeled on the wet bottom of the boat, and adjusting his position, sat down, not easy in the confined space. Susanna gripped the edge of the boat and leant back a little. The man bent his head between her thighs, and Susanna went on as she had began, "I want to sleep with you, wake with you, hold your hand in my dreams, let's leave here forever. For me nothing matters, I have no regrets..."

The man sat up, looked up at her and in the easy nonchalant look he gave her (thus housewives look up from washing the vegetables if the postman or a neighbour knocks) there was something mocking, an infernal, ridiculing impudence, with nothing to vindicate it. For the first time Susanna felt a little ashamed (although that word was hardly new to them)... Peter Bakics only stroked her face and urged, "Be a little patient, we must wait for the right moment."

Susanna was on the verge of tears. The thorns on the rose of patience dug deep at his evasive reply. Then an unusual discord arose between her body and spirit. Her usual jubilant love-making was marred by her hard-edged impatience which trampled down more fiercely on her wounded feelings. She knew she could not sever herself from the man. From this intentional, unintentional, yielding yet protesting state evolved a new and sensual mix of anger and self-pity, something like that, yes... Then suddenly her inner turmoil subsided, and her hurt flowed away as water from a wide-mouthed jug. Tumbling, her empty soul arrived at a point of no return, leaving only sky, the thinning, drifting, death-white clouds, the bushes by the lake-shore, their extending branches holding out white and red berries, their rustling leaves, their wide, yellow leaves. Somewhere, very far away, her sister's snapping voice broke the gentle murmur of nature, but it did not matter... Her fingers ploughed and caressed the man's rich hair...

Ferenc shut his eyes.

He waited for Thurzó to send for him once more, in vain. As Maria had once waited in vain. The family hopes now hung on Thurzó, but everybody had contradictory expectations. And Ferenc kept his distance.

They fried the freshly caught fish and ate them from large pewter platters - without him.

He waited. When at last he heard footsteps along the passage, he opened the door a crack.

It was Susanna coming with a burning candle in her hand. Her beauty now drew all to itself with an opulent and overwhelming attraction. Her figure had not filled out, but her uncovered shoulders seemed more fleshly, and her green eyes were Sargassos that drew all gazers into their sensual depths.

"Come in. I want to say something to you," he began.

But Susanna obviously did not wish to enter.

"All right, here then."

And he began softly, despair breaking in his throat, to say believe me, Susanna, he was the most oppressed worm on earth, everything had happened as her father had predicted after their marriage...the words tumbled out of him... "Things will get better, just let me get closer to you, I'm certain you don't love Peter Bakics, you cannot love him, you just need him. I understand, I will never reproach you for anything, you can be certain of it.

Let's forget, let's go back to Szklabinya, or wherever you want, perhaps we will even have children..."

Watching and listening to him face to face (this had not happened for a long time), Susanna was touched by pity and frustration, and a terrible curiosity awoke in her from which she just as quickly shrank away. The vague, transient and lunatic idea of what would happen if they were together again, truly cleaving together for eternity and recapturing the lost chances of another life. Who would not be tempted to seize the half-glimmering hope of a new destiny, mirage though it may be?

"Leave me, I am tired now. We will talk of these things later," she said and turned to leave.

But Ferenc clutched her arm. Even the most brutal rejection would have affected him less than this potential assent, this floundering, familiar and patronising postponement, which to him seemed like a cynical throw of the dice.

"You shouldn't have gone fishing!"

"Why shouldn't I have gone?"

"You displayed yourself in front of everybody with your lover," he said, using this expression for the first time, at least to her face.

"I went with my sister," replied Susanna (the faces of the tiny angels of innocence in the heavens could not have been as pale as hers).

Then Ferenc Révay said, "From tomorrow you will remain in your room!" He added, "I will lock you in."

But Susanna, in her anger, found a reply...that he was too late, she had spoken with Thurzó about initiating a divorce.

The Master forbade the Mistress to go fishing, but she went anyway. So there it was, unambiguous and completely logical...

When he hit her, Susanna, strangely enough, hardly defended herself. As she was pushed against the wall, she simply kept looking into his eyes, as if opening herself to the blows, and repeated, "I'm not afraid of you" - like one child to another in the hot sand, the more afraid the louder the assertion... Then she laughed, but this laughter - so said a spying witness - was like an enticing and moaning bird-song which she (the witness) had heard only one other time in her life, by the cemetery fence when she had hidden herself in the tall mallows and luxuriant undergrowth.

Then Susanna suddenly gripped her husband's robe, pulled at it, and tore the light material, leaving Ferenc standing there in humiliating nakedness, paralysed. He gazed astonished at his wife's face, into the glimmering hollows of her eyes, and waited as if demanding something from her. Then, without even moving to cover the most private parts of his body, he raised his hands towards her.

Strangling is so like loving, how easy to cross the border from an embrace to a slaying. Encircling the neck, that sensitive and vulnerable part of the body in the powerful joined arcs of male hands, perhaps this has a particularly provocative effect? And do not the panting of approaching death, the face-to-face struggle, the final slackening of the grip recall erotic movements? Perhaps, perhaps... We cannot claim to understand such things.

"Why didn't the Mistress expire under the Master's tightening hold? Sheer luck, I should say..."

That is the ultimate question. Ferenc Révay himself did not know the answer, or what he would have done in the moments that followed, if the candle, which had fallen to the ground, still burning beneath their feet, had not caught his robe (torn or not, it made no difference now). At first it was only a spark, then the fire caught the material with a subtle crack. He tried to tear it off, but - this episode is vague and even the prying witness was unsure ("if I hadn't seen it with my own eyes, I would not have believed it") - the burning robe still hung on him in red, glowing streams of lava, a froth from its wrinkles and folds sliding down his body, the tongues of flame clutching at his head, shooting higher, with his face and loins lit up in the white light, wax white (Arcimboldo, Arcimboldo...), even as alarmed relations appeared (who had called them?) at the end of the passageway, where the stairs descended under a narrow arch. They came running in a throng, pressing into the narrow corridor, their necks extended, a wild torchlight procession led by the Imperial Councillor, Thurzó himself. And while the secret witness turned to watch this crowd scene, the great erupting flames subsided, leaving Ferenc Révay's body unmarked where he stood. The singed remains of the burned robe lay on the ground near him. His hair, wet and bedraggled, fell over his dazed, grey face.

György Thurzó went to Susanna, who lay on the floor. He slipped his hands under her neck, raised her head a little and then saw the tiny finger marks in their distinct contours and red stripes. "My God," he said, and no more.

"She is alive," he added after a pause; and he carefully returned the insensible head to the floor. He stood up, ordered that Susanna be taken directly upstairs to her sister's apartment and finally turned to Ferenc Révay, saying this would be best for everybody.

This last seemed to break Ferenc's trance. He did not say anything, he just smiled, if that term can be used for the strange, veiled spasm of his eyes and mouth. Had not Thurzó urged the move from Szklabinya to Holics in exactly the same terms: "This would be best for everybody"? Who was this everybody and how could the best be found in this wretchedness suspended between eternity and zero, commonly called life and death? The situation amused him. But his expression simply frightened the others, as they hovered over Susanna's swooning body. They perceived the sure signs of madness in him.

So Thurzó once again had to arrange matters, and they led Ferenc into his room, where he was made to drink restorative teas and get under the covers...

He obeyed.

Peter Révay stayed with his brother. He sat by the head of the bed with his hands patiently in his lap, asking over and over how to set things right. It could not be put off any longer... He looked fearfully, surreptitiously, at his brother. Peter had never borne easily the grave air of the sick-room. In his youth he had fled from his father's deathbed; but now as an adult, though he would have liked to leave, his compassion summoned him back and made him attempt to talk to his brother, if it would help... But he found he could not get through.

Thurzó meanwhile went to Peter Bakics ("It would be best if you heard from me what has happened!").

It seemed the servants had forgotten to enlighten him. Completely unaware, Bakics was waiting in a dreamlike state. He would have preferred not to go to bed alone; and just as he was musing on how some people change, Thurzó came in, locked the door behind him and put the key in his pocket.

Cautiously (as if the news were some sort of gift) Thurzó told Bakics his tale. At first he said only that Susanna's husband had given her a good hiding, nothing serious, and that for safety's sake she had been taken to her sister's. Only later did he add that Ferenc had tried to strangle her.

It was very unfortunate, Thurzó went on, but Peter Bakics must remain where he was, not moving from his room. Things must not be made worse. He continued (skilfully smoothing over the past and present with liberal applications of the future..."the hypnotic future" which we know so well), so be it, if there must be a divorce, let there be a divorce! But not conducted in a vulgar way that would merely debase all of us... Just now, however, it would be *for the best* if Peter Bakics left at dawn, somewhere, anywhere, no matter, just for a few days while tempers were allowed to cool ("I know what I ask of you is not easy...").

"First I must go up to Susanna," said Peter Bakics.

Thurzó replied that this wish was understandable, but unfortunately not acceptable, and he muttered something about dire consequences (the muttering was supposed to convey that Thurzó would rather not have asked this of him).

Peter did not say a word, just waited in front of the locked door. Thurzó took the key from his pocket, also in silence, and gave it to him, clasping his hand as a sign of good will. Thurzó waited... Let Bakics see for himself, as he wished, that Susanna was all right. But then he, Thurzó, who wished to remain a mediator and not a back-stabbing, false friend on either side, would be forced to withdraw his support... He would bear no ill will towards Peter, but the circumstances would compel him.

Then Peter Bakics said, "You'll promise to explain everything to Susanna?"

"Naturally," said Thurzó, gently and confidingly squeezing his arm.

37

So Susanna was left to recover from her injuries with only her sister for company.

In her helpless state, she was at last Maria's victim. Maria went through everything, their father's peace, disturbed both in life and death, the polluted morals of her children (even those still to be born), dirty fingers on every white page of the album of innocence, shame to Klara (nails in her coffin), most of all the threat to her husband Peter Révay, this stinking scandal jeopardised his position at court...

The worst of it was that Susanna had to depend on Maria for everything: food, drink, medicine, clean linen..., although she had to admit that in all these respects Maria was very conscientious. Maria tried to think of every-thing, surely unaware that poison to the soul and cures to the body cancel each other out...

One day Thurzó sent everyone out of the sick-room, settled on the edge of the bed, and asked her about everything, and in detail about her physical state, shaking his head while clouds of anxiety passed gently across his forehead.

"I understand you, I do not condemn you, believe me! Indeed I would like to help you arrange a peaceful divorce." The gestures of a Pharisee came naturally to him, either stroking his beard or rubbing his hands. But "in the interests of the case" (this was one of his favourite expressions when bridge-building or campaign-ing at court), it was important that Susanna be strong and bottle-up her lovesick spirit - no, no need to be alarmed, only for a short while - and move back with her husband as soon as possible. Because as all the world knows, it is impossible to steer a ship in a storm. (So Thurzó produced his reasons like rabbits out of a magician's hat.) "Because you know, my little one, that I know about the world, do you not? Or perhaps you are afraid? Don't be afraid, if your husband lifts one finger to hurt you, you only need send word and I will come, I will drop everything and take you with me in my own carriage to my wife!"

"In my own carriage" - he repeated this several times

with emphasis, as if everything depended on it.

Strewing the fire with ashes.

He then went to bid farewell to Ferenc Révay.

As if he were just going to bid farewell...

Only after exchanging a few idle sentences about his wife Elizabeth Czobor's health, the state of the roads, and struggles for the throne, did Thurzó mention that he had spoken to Susanna about her intention to divorce, but it appeared that it was by no means irrevocably settled ("my senses do not often lie..."). He told Ferenc that tenderness and open-heartedness would be helpful, "Approach her, entice her home with sweet words..."

Then Thurzó bade farewell and embraced Ferenc, squeezing his arm confidingly, and hurried off to pack.

Ferenc stood outside the doorway, hesitating, then he went to her with outstretched arms, "I come to you in love, my sweet Susanna..." So he began. Thurzó's advice, it seemed, had not fallen on barren soil!

Since they had brought her up here, Susanna had not really tried to get up. She hid in her musty nest, as if her own body smells, her sweat and her pain were the covers that protected and isolated her from the world.

But now she ran out of the room, down the slippery stairs, and out of the house in her nightgown, stepping barefoot on the bare earth. She went straight into Peter Bakics' apartments, where György Thurzó was preparing to depart.

Susanna fell on her knees before him (he was just pressing his hat to his head) and sobbing, begged him to take her with him right now in his carriage. She would be his servant, his slave, only take her away from here!

At this all Thurzó's honey-tongued meekness fell from him like roast meat from the bone. The room around them, filled with trunks, their lids open and overbrimming with heaped-up clothes (the servants would have to sit on them to get them closed) was now a fortress of impatience. Thurzó stepped back from Susanna and instead of helping her to rise, began to shout quite unchivalrously, "You should be ashamed of yourself! Go back to your husband! Right away!"

There lay the knife with its long narrow blade and heavy ornamental hilt. (Why did Thurzó insist on breakfasting with precisely this knife, not something more suitable? We see how the tree of personality stretches out its branches at such moments.) There it lay on the table, among the crumbs, chewed bones and spat-out bits of fat, offering itself.

Susanna picked it up, as she was now truly desperate.

Perhaps it was the form and weight of it that made her hold it so clumsily in her hands, as if it were a violin bow. She turned it towards herself, then applied it to her pale inner wrist, at the fork of the blue veins, at their cross, repeatedly.

"I stood there like stone," so they would say afterwards. And, unmannerly as it may seem, they stood perplexed until the blood dripped, fat provocative drops, staining the velvet cover of the Imperial Councillor's favourite coffer. Only then did Thurzó cry out to one of the two servants (they would later quarrel bitterly as to which one):

"What are you gaping at? Take it away from her!"

But it was not necessary. Susanna, now limp as a rag-doll, had noticed Peter Bakics' clothes were in one of the trunks. Dropping the knife, she went down on her knees, or rather sank to the ground, pressed her face to his coat and cried. Meanwhile agile fingers held her wrist, binding fast the cut veins, but the blood seeped through, so that they had to wind still more bandages around it.

She continued weeping and calling Peter Bakics' name. Then Ferenc, who had been standing for a time a little way off, said, "You would do better to call on God!" but to what purpose he did not say.

As if he had given them a signal, the onlookers, both inside the room and without, began rhythmically repeating Thurzó's words, "Go back! Go back! Go back!" And everyone at once seemed to have latched on to this new mood, "You must go back!"

Then they took her to her room, forcefully gripping her hands and legs. Not to her sister's, but to her husband's chambers. Ferenc Révay would have entreated Thurzó to stay longer in order to speak with him; but Thurzó turned towards him nervously and by way of farewell whispered in his ear, "Skilfully, not by force!"

György Thurzó called for his horses in visible panic; he did not want to spend another minute with his dear relations. As his carriage turned towards the castle gates, he shouted to the ardently waving Maria, "I've seen enough!"

So coldly, so severely he spoke that Maria's narrow mouth froze in the midst of her soft, pandering smile.

38

From then on Ferenc kept Susanna locked in her room, with a guard outside the door (skilfully, skilfully). The room had to be her privy as well. Bread and water were the only rations he allowed her.

Of course, Peter Bakics came by secret means to hear of this. But wherever he turned to slander Thurzó in his despair, his audience simply slunk away.

In a rage Ferenc destroyed Susanna's room, although she herself was merely pushed aside. He did not touch her, now that the affair had seeped irrevocably out of those four walls (at such times madness and sober reason

concur very well). It was the same old story of broken
furniture, although he now had an axe to split the chests
with. He found one of the men's costumes and waved it
triumphantly from one end of the castle to the other, as if
it were a flag. Nobody could understand what the
garment signified in his confused spirit, denial or proof,
but nobody dared to ask. He carried it down to the
courtyard under Susanna's window ("She will never need
this again, let her lover make her another"). First he
ripped it with a sword then set fire to it. Later he winkled
out the inflammable parts from the ashes - buttons and
clasps all deformed and sooty - gathered them together
and locked them away, along with the withered grass
stems.

"There will be a catastrophe," Maria kept saying,
adding indignantly that she did not want to witness it (as
if she had booked seats for a comedy and was being
treated to a tragedy instead). One day not long before
Christmas, when the approach of the first snow could be
felt in the silky air, still lamenting and complaining she
packed up her children and the last of her things. She did
not even say goodbye to Ferenc Révay.

"It is better that she is gone," he said. He immediately
sent for the presumed messenger boys (among them the
poor, industrious Daniel) to be shackled. Then he went
to Susanna, walking with dignity past the guards he had
placed at her door, and with a new coldness, without
salutation, said, "Now sit here at the table and write
down what I dictate..."

Carelessly he waved a blank sheet he had brought.
Susanna was to take the blame for everything, her
mocking infidelity and the breakdown of their marriage.

But it seemed he could not maintain his tight-lipped
dignity, because before Susanna could answer, he added
that he could deny her bread and water from tomorrow.

But Susanna was already preparing herself for an

annulment, and she was practising: that she would swear a thousand times to anybody and everybody, her hand on the Holy Bible, that between her and Peter Bakics was only the most noble of familial relationships, purity and honour and nothing else.

Ferenc, as a Lutheran, expected nothing more than such lies from the Papish oaths of corpulent priests under orders from the Vatican.

But a few days later he tried again to extort a confession from Susanna, in an entirely different tone. Instead of threats he asked, he begged her in the name of justice, "Why must everything be yours and nothing mine? You will be happy and I will remain here bereft, I have lost my wife, do you want me also to lose my honour?"

Susanna stubbornly refused.

"Then there remains nothing else but to kill you."

"You are too cowardly to do that either," said Susanna with a wave of her hand.

A hyena's laugh could not have been more harsh to Ferenc Révay's ears. Wet snow dripped off the roof and every single drop spelt the words, "It is the end."

That was the last time they saw each other alive.

39

The kidnappers came in soft felt boots (on January 27th, 1607, to be exact) sometime before midnight.

Removing bricks which had been loosened in advance.

Susanna was wearing a cloak which Peter Bakics had got from the German Captain of the Guard. It had cost a pretty penny.

Only the snow, the pale moon and the cold light of a few winter stars lit the night.

She stumbled over a stone and split her heel-bone (the doctor later confirmed this), but at the time she only felt slight nausea. No matter...she had to make it to the carriage.

Later Ferenc (who knows how he discovered the accident?) could not insist enough, as if Susanna had broken her neck - behold how God's thunderbolt had struck down the wicked!

But the truth was that the German cloak was too long for her and she was nervous. Once inside the carriage, Susanna and her two serving maids were accompanied by Bakics and his men on horseback (Why did her servants go with her? A sense of adventure? Fear of being left behind?) Inside it was not much warmer than out. They shivered, and Susanna's foot hurt very much. Coming alongside, Peter stroked and caressed her cold hands, breathing on the tip of her nose as he kissed it. Although they had to flee, Peter Bakics was now calm and in good humour, his eyes shone and he laughed. At last! At last! This was the task, this was the summons which God had created for him, for Peter Bakics, his chosen fate, for him alone!

While they travelled through populated regions they did not dare light the torches, and in front of the carriage a man with a lamp wound round with rags lit the way. Clouds later flooded the clear winter sky, low-hanging cotton wool clouds, and in the thick fog the horses stumbled blindly, the wind rose and kept blowing out the torches they had at last dared to light. They took a roundabout route ("through terribly evil places" it would later be told), so that in every village on the way somebody had to be awakened, pulled from their beds to guide them through the fords, thickets and lanes. ("We went along roads where our guides held aloft torches on pitchforks, and the only light we had was just five paces ahead of us.")

Once they thought they heard gunfire in the distance. (This always comes into kidnappers' ballads, doesn't it?) The horses crossed ice-cold waters, only shying away from the marshy swamps where everybody feared the mud.

But they got through it all.

Towards dawn, that unfriendly, misty winter dawn, Margit Bakics waited by one of Detreko's outer ramparts. She welcomed them in a six-horse carriage, having (as usual) brought along musicians. So they went with celebratory music among the sleeping houses, and by the time people were roused and out of bed, only the stumps of their torches could be seen where the travellers had thrown them down at the road edge, in gardens and terraces. Without thinking, the townspeople carefully stowed them away. (Later some came into the possession of Ferenc Révay as material proof.)

As it grew lighter the number of watchers increased, and jokes and pleasantries went round the crowd. Of course everyone wanted to know:

"Have they brought priests?"

"Of course they have!"

"I thought it strange that there was music for the priest during the journey, but nowadays who can tell?"

When they at last arrived at the impregnable Detreko Castle itself, and the inner gates (happy gates) closed behind them, is it necessary to give the details of the joy the lovers felt then?

Strange bed, but familiar hands.

Strange faces endearingly (curiously) peeped at them as if measuring them up, whispering and sometimes averting their eyes. The same countenances they had encountered at Holics.

Margit Bakics stayed with them. In fact she had

brought an entire wardrobe to compensate "our little runaway" for what she had had to leave behind in Ferenc's mad, wicked hands.

Happiness, happiness, the clash of Hymen's cymbals, heavenly kisses, hymns of nightingales, Hyperion's reign in the shining citadel, the whole alliterative trumpeting of happiness... But how long can happiness be preserved? How long would the feast of freedom last between them?

Possibly for a long time.

Surely Susanna was happy, truly happy in the high castle of Detreko (given the state of her past...).

Or is it possible that that shuttlecock, the soul (not for the first time going *incognito* in the guise of perfectly satisfied love), just at the decisive moment of arrival had already set out on the slow return journey?

How long will love persist after the siege of blind suffering has at last been lifted? How long can passion subsist on a meagre diet of ordinary sensations, intimate silences, on the sparrow seed of secure possession? These questions must be asked.

But now is not the time.

40

Ferenc Révay silently and accusingly eyed the empty rooms. For hours he said not a word, just roamed the ghostly chambers until the dread of what had happened broke within him and burst open that which until now had been bound hand and foot, the free current of his emotions. He began to roar and curse.

He also fled in his own way. First he began to write a fanatic stream of letters to all his relations, close persons of rank, informing them of his terrible shame, and asking help from virtually the whole world for a "true restoration of order".

He primarily sent these letters of complaint to aristocrats, bishops, preachers, scribes and courtiers throughout the country who did not already know the story, thus confirming the reports which had been circulating for months in dainty circles.

He awaited their replies. István Illésházy's letter was the most painful disappointment, though the Palatine did send a long and courteous missive, neither sparing his precious time nor caring for his own weariness, it seemed.

"Believe me, if a married couple do not understand each other, a stranger (with the greatest will in the world) cannot make them come to any greater understanding.

"If Susanna Forgách is truly the lecherous, debased person that you paint her to be, then be grateful they have taken her away from you!

"Perhaps you yourself were lured into sin, you must think about this also... Better that she committed a sin, than if you had killed her in a fit of passion.

"She has destroyed herself enough. You are not the one who has offended God's Commandments; thus it would be best if you wait in calm and peace until the next Parliamentary sitting. Do not forget, you are not the first nor the last to suffer injustice...

"Everything depends on which side you are on." (An amazing change, is it not?)

Ferenc Révay set about gathering proof. Feverishly, pedantically he wanted to hold the facts in his hand, to discover the "whole" truth, to drain it to the dregs (as if there were a greater truth than that those two, Susanna Forgách and Peter Bakics, hand in hand on a frosty night, walked out together...).

To determine and name the facts. Everything depended on this!

So that in the great opening scene Peter Bakics steps forward as a seducer or perhaps a rescuer, who from pity or carnal desire, bears down...does he rescue Susanna Forgách chivalrously or steal her deceitfully?

This had to be decided at the outset, before anything could go further.

He set up a domestic court, calling it his *judicium privatum.* Even sometimes referring to it as his *judicium extraordinarium.*

Naturally, he was the president. He sat in an armchair behind a long table in the centre of the room. Beside him ordinary chairs were set for the other members of the court.

To Ferenc's right sat his old accomplice and sometime turncoat, Janos Kutsera.

Next to him sat a fire-stoker called Vavra, who had seen and heard virtually everything while attending to his duties, and who felt personally affronted on his Master's behalf, because his own fiancée, a certain Barbara, had spent one of those famed midsummer nights with the scribe István, yes, yes...in a word he was somewhat prejudiced against the eloping couple.

On the president's left sat Kata Káldi, a noblewoman. She had invited the lovers on the infamous fishing trip, and had many times been a guest of theirs. She did not really understand how she had become involved, although she had dressed for the extraordinary occasion, in waves of lace and ribbons.

Beside her huddled one of Maria Forgách's old women, her intimates, one of the two old crows.

The witnesses had to stand to give their testimonies. Though there were hundreds of them, the hearings slid along quickly. Naturally, of Bakics' men and Susanna's servants only those who had changed sides remained at Holics... Need we say anything further about the usual exaggerations of turncoat zeal?

However, Ferenc became extremely irritated with his fellow judges. First because Kutsera carped and queried, labouring to see what was behind completely transparent events. He fussed and pestered about facts - for example about the man's suit of clothes - anything he suspected Ferenc was particularly interested in. Kutsera was convinced he was right about the change of clothes. With sleuth-like tenacity he questioned again and again those who had seen the two women when they rode out; the escape was carried out by moonlight and candle-light...that proved his Master had not found the red suit but the garnet one, and that Susanna had escaped in the red one. But when Ferenc himself produced a garnet rag which they had found in one of the streams along the road, Kutsera asserted that was just the colour red would turn if it had been in sunlight or in the open air for some time.

Vavra continually brought the subject round to his own preoccupations. In his eyes the personalities had some-how become blurred, as if he were sitting at his own trial against Barbara, not Ferenc Révay's. He was always trying to bring the proceedings around to the obscene summer "orgies".

Kata Káldi offended by giggling at the most unfortunate moments. To her the whole thing was merely exciting. When they debated the riddle of the clothes, she interrupted to say that she thought it was neither red nor garnet because, if a woman in the sweet midnight hour escapes on the arm of her lover from her lawful husband (this was a little exaggerated!), she would be sure not to wear men's clothes, for breeches close off all that which a skirt does not... Then she started to laugh shamelessly.

Mrs Nemeth, the black crone, who also was not really following events, merely intoned from time to time that it was all the same whether sluts flaunted themselves in red or blue... "I have lived long enough to know," thus she dismissed it all. When she was not speaking she was trying to pluck out a stubborn hair from the corner of her mouth, at the same time muttering to herself, "Whores, tarts, sluts..." To her it made no difference, the formula held true.

41

In the opening scene of what seemed like the final act, Ferenc Révay's case appeared strong.

It was not as if the nosegay of proof he had prepared (or the unanimous verdict of his private court) concerned anyone in Archduke Mátyás' circle. Nor was a public legal case of interest to him, not at all. The favourable winds blew in from an entirely different quarter. For just as Ferenc's bundle of evidence arrived at the Archduke's, clever hands were preparing to rewrite the rules for the game of power.

Even as the last embers of freedom were dying away, Ferenc Forgách (who had meanwhile become an Imperial governor and Archbishop of Esztergom) was attempting to put the cowering forces of the Counter-Reformation on their feet. A little known but important event of the period was his letter to the Pope in which the archbishop sought to inform His Holiness that the alliance which Archduke Mátyás had made with Protestants had happened without the knowledge and consent of either him or the Catholic priesthood.

For the present, however, Mátyás thought his Protestant treaty important. His tenacious brother was still cringing in Hradzsin, and Mátyás could allow only tiny fissures to break his mask.

We cannot be at all surprised - if we recognise the nature of those volatile times - that the prospects for and opinions of divorce changed from moment to moment. As it was not really the custom to write openly about political aims, the national colours, anything which the occasion presented were used as substitutes. So that from this time Protestant and Catholic, religious tolerance and the Counter-Reformation lined up against each other by proxy through the plaintiffs and defendants in a private case. We must not wonder it was the Catholic clergy who lined up on the side of the adulteress! (The inconvenient fact of lust was of course tactfully covered up...)

So here is another paradox of our Hungarian Romance, its bizarre finale (but does not life itself consist of such slips?), that freedom of religiom and freedom of love pirouetted into battle against each other, just because the fickle rules of the game demanded it.

György Thurzó zealously espoused Ferenc Révay's case (against his own "beautiful sister"...but let's leave this). There were assorted power-plays: Mátyás in an Imperial decree forbade the Holy See from meddling in Susanna Forgách's divorce and transferred the case to the Imperial Court, where Ferenc Révay was plaintiff. The clergy cried out, the archbishop grumbled and haughtily declared Susanna's innocence; the Hungarian Protestants (that is, the aristocracy) eagerly lined up behind Ferenc Révay. Ingenious punishments for carnal sin were invented, and campaigning took place on all sides with feverish excitement.

The hullabaloo subsided only when Mátyás (Thurzó had pressed for this) summoned the regional counties, aristocrats and commanders: "We summon you in the name of Our Imperial brother to satisfy Our good supporters and as a warning to others..." Then the flood was checked, because no one was really willing to lay siege to Detreko. They shrugged their shoulders and sounded out their neighbours. The decision was unanimous: Bakics' castle was impossible to conquer by siege.

Ferenc Révay was, of course, deeply offended. But he took Illésházy's letter to heart and prepared a charge to be brought before Parliament. Thus a petition went round the aristocracy for signatures to enact a statute against the adulterers. The proposal was accepted, everybody necessary signed it, twelve in all, except - who? - István Illésházy, on the understandable grounds that he had already used his best offices in the case. Later he - the only Protestant to do so - openly took the clergy's side (one howling dervish in the night was plainly enough).

Parliament opened in Pozsony. In the same high chamber where the extraordinary Court had sat for Illésházy's trial not so long ago.

There the 1608/26 Statute was constructed, without any loopholes, out of three clauses:

That the great Lord Bakics had snatched Susanna Forgách from Holics Castle out of mad, passionate love, doing this and this (we know the rest!).

That it was necessary to summon the sinners before the Palatine, because if it was overlooked they would commit similar evils, setting a precedent for others, and that they should be imprisoned (the logic of the Illésházy case crept in here too).

That a sentence must be delivered against them through an extraordinary statute, and that the sentence be executed in full...

Ferenc Révay was triumphant, finally finding himself in a circle of sympathetic friends. When he caught sight of Bakics, who also came to the Parliament, he spat and everybody applauded.

Bakics sent a sad letter home to Susanna, saying that, for the time being, she should not leave Detreko's rock-clad safety. She was even frightened to go down into the courtyard, where threatening letters kept arriving, including several from Thurzó, replete with Latin tags and words like "treachery" and "deceit":

"Insolent seducer, withdraw now, because otherwise, *punica fides,* you will be burnt at the stake!"

Publicly Bakics countered every challenge, but privately he sent his fears to Susanna: "Here I am, but I will return home. They are bringing a law against us. Everybody has turned their backs on me; there are those who will not even return my greeting. I am ostracised, it seems..."

But why did he not produce Ferenc Révay's list of offences? The temptation was surely great. But he did not do it, because the lovers now adhered strictly to the instructions of Ferenc Forgách, who forbade wasting valuable gunpowder on unfavourable ground... "Patience, patience, let them burn themselves out, then we shall come forward!"

To these confident lines (addressed to Susanna) the archbishop always added a few reproving moral lashings: "I protected you from such things in your childhood. I warned your poor father more than once, but if God does not open a man's eyes, what can one do?"

42

At the first sitting of the parliamentary court, the accused did not appear. Peter Bakics sent an apology that he was ill. They judged him to be in contempt of court.

Then an ecclesiastical court summoned Ferenc Révay to come before it. Now it was he who did not appear. So they charged him as well - with the same crime, naturally.

But Ferenc did not send any apology. On the contrary,

he declared (the sight of imminent victory easily moves a man to enthusiasms), To hell with the Holy See! To hell with legates and nuncios! Only the country's legal courts could sentence a Hungarian!

Since being forced to leave his closed and hidden world, he - who throughout his life had slunk away, keeping his distance from flag-waving and shows of faith - had assumed a loud, indeed a boastful manner in the lists of public life. Only when another summons arrived from the Holy See (a philippic accompanied by threatened punishments of one thousand gold coins, plus excommunication) did he write an alarmed letter to Ferenc Forgách.

The archbishop was in a merciful mood, "I grant you 15 days grace" (doubtless Ferenc Forgách felt he would not need to carry out the threats, or wait so long...). But he did not delude Ferenc Révay with false hope either; though perhaps the disputatious husband was seeking some.

In due course an extraordinary hearing of the ecclesiastical court was convened. Instead of Peter and Susanna only their lawyers appeared. Ferenc Forgách as an Imperial governor was appointed Prothonotary. He read out carefully, without introduction or explanation (saying it had come out of the blue), the signed document of Ferenc Révay's old sins. The archbishop stopped only to allow the startled observers a pause when he came to the part in the text where "I made her blood run, causing me perverse pleasure..." Then with theatrical indifference his glance raked the room. He waited.

Ferenc Révay's lawyer blinked numbly at his client as he tried in vain to refute and protest every new accusation. In that silence now buzzing with deceit, the wind had truly changed...

Public opinion, which had protected Ferenc Révay so far, now felt swindled. Even though its leaders might stay silent, the chameleon public changed a cuckold into a sadist, an adulteress into a martyr, and a lecher into a hero. Old fossil notions were pushed off the shelf. From one pole to the other, and what lies between? The whole of life. *Die ganze welt,* no less.

This change of mood was fed by the fact that Ferenc's protests did not touch on details of his own confession, but on all existing and conceivable allegations he could make about the other party.

When the judges, shaking their heads and proceeding from assertion to assertion, attempted to question him, he evaded them, saying that he did not contest the kidnapping of the woman.

He was afraid of the particulars.

How could he have guessed that, years later, when Peter Bakics spoke for the first time about what the true situation between Ferenc and his wife had been (or had not been...), everybody would just laugh? There were those who would see it as a good joke and others, as a tasteless one (an unnecessary trophy...). But no one believed it.

43

A period of light relief followed in the affair. Peter Bakics and Susanna Forgách prepared to take a solemn oath supported by fifty witnesses each, vowing that whatever snooping, derisive candle might be held over the snow-white bed, nothing objectionable had happened between them there!

As time passed Ferenc Révay tirelessly pursued his own truth. He proposed new lines of inquiry for the judges, namely, "What clothes did Susanna Forgách wear to Detreko? Did she venture out from Detreko, and if so in what clothes?" He quite astonished everybody with his nonsense.

Meanwhile, however, the full complement of a hundred aristocratic witnesses was difficult to get together. To be honest, those who promised cooperation were a somewhat dubious company.

Finally ("as it is impossible elsewhere..."), the swearing was ordered to take place discreetly in Ferenc Forgách's own archbishopric...

Thus in March of 1611 the hundred witnesses duly gathered in Pozsony. But then they dispersed, went on a spree, so it was not easy to round them up for the ceremony in Saint Martin's Cathedral on the seventh of that month, in the very church of the coronation of Hungarian kings, which had been full to bursting since early morning, with spectators coming even from Vienna.

First there was a great mass (never was the liturgy invoked in a stranger cause). Then all one hundred lined up before the altar - half standing behind Susanna and half behind Peter Bakics, marking time with mocking faces (but a little moved in spite of themselves), in their motley furs and odd hats. They waited with an indecently loud hawking of throats and clanking of swords.

At a signal they all turned towards the chancel, where the judges sat, and each witness swore on his religion and his life, first on behalf of Peter Bakics (also roaring out his own name when it came to his turn), his rooted opposition to all the charges, point by point:

"I, XY, swear on the Holy Trinity and the one true God that Peter Bakics, when the plaintiff Ferenc Révay was out or away attending to his business, did not fall in carnal love with Susanna Forgách, did not with predetermined, calculated evil play cards with her, flirt with her, pass the time in forbidden kisses or embraces..." and then each one, raising his voice a little, glancing straight at the judges, fixing them with his eyes, restraining any mockery (this took a certain skill...) added "Not guilty!" and then a second time, heaving a sigh like a weak echo, repeated, "Not guilty!"

The text of the oath was absurd, but Susanna was nevertheless so frightened she was almost sick. At the same time the tittering in the pews (with lowered voices in deference to the holiness of the place), the pomp, the rich altar with its reliquary, the comings and goings of lawyers, all lent a festive mood to the performance.

Only Ferenc Révay's lawyer shouted out in the middle of it, that a sentence had been left out of the charges...

So Susanna stood at the head of her supporters, feeling faint. Did she manage to smile despite her shame? Or perhaps, only as the ceremony progressed did shame well within her. In truth she was more ashamed than even her husband would have been had he been there. To have to stand here in the dim, pious light of the coronation church, with its smell of sanctity, close by the font and the altar, among those marble Madonnas, proud Madonnas, ecstatic Madonnas and their plump baby Jesuses, and have to confess in everybody's hearing.

Though she recalled when they had arrived in Pozsony and her cousin had embraced her, as they went up to the Primate's palace (up those stairs smelling of celibacy and men's bodies), as they passed among the whispering reverences, the vacant looks and bows of papal officials going down slowly or hurrying upwards, she had said, "I am afraid," and the archbishop had replied there was nothing to be afraid about... She found it interesting and also comforting that he knew exactly what she, Susanna, was thinking. Because he did not go on to say do not be afraid, it will succeed, but whispered to her, "What you must do is merely a harmless white lie, a forgivable sin..." And then what childish relief, what open love had swept over Susanna. How delightful it would be to nestle against her cousin as she had done in childhood, to ask him about King Mátyás' disguised visit of old, about that fleeting masque of love and power; and to confess how she had overheard... But as she had turned towards him, she noticed for the first time (or rather for the first time permitted herself the discovery?) that their features were distinctly similar: those almond-shaped, moist, large eyes, the high, but softly rounded forehead... Why had she noticed it only at that moment?

That evening Peter Bakics rented an inn to entertain the hundred witnesses and celebrate their victory. He drank a lot, his glance was aflame; he laughed, opening his arms to accept their congratulations and good wishes - and yet it seemed as if his great joy did not come from within. Everything about him was tense, as if he were about to flee.

The guests drummed on the tables. Someone vomited in the corner, and it was quickly scattered with ash. Others clumsily came to blows, rolling on the floor. Susanna involuntarily looked out the window (had a horse neighed in the darkness? she had to laugh). She asked Peter Bakics to come home, to their quarters in the Primate's palace, in proper separate rooms, of course, only come... But the man replied that he had to stay.

Where once the childish sprite in her soul would have danced and clapped for joy, now she discovered that she was far removed from the celebrations.

"Don't you feel well?" asked Peter Bakics anxiously.

"I am tired," said Susanna. This is how she explained to herself her strange indifference.

Only later, back home at Detreko, as they pulled the covers over their naked bodies and Peter Bakics blew out the candles, bringing darkness and silence like a gift, did Susanna remark as she leaned her head on the man's warm neck, that perhaps the last few years had all been a

great lie (a necessary lie, nevertheless)... Perhaps that is
what had worn her out so much.

Perhaps.

44

Ferenc Révay moved back to Szklabinya. To the scene of
former wanderings and tormented thoughts.

He forbade any baby born in his domain to be
christened with the sinners' names. He also lit mourning
candles in Susanna's former room, as if he had two wives,
one to mourn and one to hate. As if he kept separate the
distant and the recent past. His thirtieth birthday passed
in solitude.

He corresponded with Maria for a while. She conscientiously sent him any news or gossip. Bakics, she informed
him, increasingly spent his time in the local taverns,
lounging about and seemingly delighted to chat with
anyone. She wrote that recently he had been heard to
declare that his great love arose from great pity ("God
knows what kind of love this is!").

And how once Bakics had brought for Susanna from
Vienna wonderful silks and laces. But when he had
spread them before her, Susanna only cried. After long
questioning (her eyes were reportedly riveted on the
cross of one of Detreko's narrow windows - of course
this was construed as a religious metaphor, however
banal) Susanna had said she would rather have gone with
Peter Bakics. (Maria: "The slow poison of tedium is
perhaps bringing her to earth, poor thing!")

And Maria reported other slurs on that lunatic love of
her sister's which had earlier appeared to be so

unshakeable. The rumour began that Peter Bakics had been tricked by the devil, if, that is, he was not the devil himself. Someone had asked him where he was keeping the wondrous Susanna. He had replied that her husband had killed and eaten her, then he rode off laughing...

But Maria made a serious error in recounting another story to Ferenc, one which, like it or not, bore the unmistakable stamp of happiness. It seems an errand boy had managed to climb a long ladder and peep through the lovers' window one Christmas Day. There were Susanna and Peter, cramped knee to knee in a wooden tub, with evident delight splashing each others' naked bodies with water... "But believe me, my poor Ferenc, a love like this will certainly not last long!"

Ferenc was of course deeply hurt and also offended by her use of "love". He thought Maria was being disloyal, using such a hurtful word; one which he had for a long time stricken from his diary of hopes and desires.

He did not write to her again.

"I am the one who stands always beside you in trouble..."

But he did not reply to this either. He had given up clutching at the straws of roles and alliances. Because the hundred yellow butterflies of his solitude had already left him to fly into another yet to be discovered sphere... (See the entomology of the soul as presented by Gabriel García Gonopteryx.)

"...the one who takes your part, walks with you, goes out to you, fluttering like the night hawk!"

But Ferenc Révay merely wrote on the margin of Maria's last attempt to console him (though making marginal notes like this was quite contrary to his custom): "Just like her sister, her wits are wandering!"

45

The remaining decade of his life Ferenc Révay filled with one unflagging struggle.

The screeching falcons of the Counter-Reformation whistled over his head, but he did not even notice them. He had only one unshakeable object: to recover Susanna Forgách - which by this time was not only hopeless *privatim* but *publice* too.

First he investigated the background and ancestry of those nobles who had taken the oath. He found among them three dubious paternities, a sheep-stealer and a wife-murderer. He knew that (historically) all three had been recruited by the archbishopric. He could thus attack the credibility of the witnesses (this kept him occupied for a long time), and of course through them the archbishop's own role in the trial. But when Ferenc Révay wrote to the archbishop that the time had come to defend the honour of the Forgách name, his enemy had simply replied that the time had come to stop pestering others.

Another strange thing that dated from this period also exercised Ferenc Révay's mind and passions. He noted that his "list of offences" included an apochryphal addition in Latin by an unknown hand, which apart from the sins listed charged him with further loathsome crimes, even sodomy! Why? Perhaps to make the rest more believable... ("In for a penny, in for a pound...all the better to eat you with" - how shall we describe these familiar artistic touches or dirty tricks?)

Sometime later he attacked the papal nuncio himself,

and in a venomous lampoon exposed how the clergy had covered up for lechery. By then seven years had passed, and this proved to be his last public action.

Not long before his death, however, he sent a bitter, complaining letter to Emperor Ferdinand (we have finished with Rudolf and his brother): "Insinuating his way into my house and confidence, hoodwinking me..." But he did not travel to either Prague or Vienna again.

That is to say, just once. Because, as the years passed, Ferenc Révay had descended still deeper into the well of the past, its dry depths from which not only smoke rose (colourful but obscuring) but from which the ancient, fabled locusts of jealousy were drawn that gnawed his soul.

He became obsessed with the musician. He sent word that he would wait for him in the gardens of the Imperial palace by the fountain. Master Basirius did not prove difficult to track down.

Cyprian bowed deeply. Yet this gesture betrayed a certain insolent ease in keeping with the rest of his appearance. Gathering the ankles of his silk trousers were daisy chains, a black velvet tunic lustrously covered his chest, and his neck sported a fringed shawl. Ferenc, discarding all his careful plans for a discreet entrée - asked the musician point-blank to say what sprang into his mind at the mention of the name Forgách.

The musician laughed..., how could he not recognise and honour the name of the Imperial governor and Prince Primate? He spoke politely but guardedly. However, Ferenc impatiently corrected him: he was not speaking of Ferenc Forgách but of his young cousin Susanna. Then Cyprian shook his head. His curled locks in trembling, descending spirals echoed the movement. Nowadays he not only painted his mouth, but his nails.

"You were her lover!" said Ferenc Révay aggressively. It seems he could think of no better rejoinder.

"Surely there's been some mistake," began the musician in all innocence. After Ferenc threatened to throw him into the near-by river bound hand and foot, however, Cyprian recalled vaguely yes, yes, in his youth he had been for a short time the court musician at Komjáti.

"In my youth...," he drawled, as brazenly as if there were no early corruptions in his eyes, something of a cosmic youth (dry stigmata, displayed brightly polished). "Don't worry, I don't eat toadstools," he murmured with a smile, as if to say goodbye.

46

Peter Révay and György Thurzó, when they mentioned this meeting, were forced to allude for the last time to the family scandal.

When news of Ferenc's antics reached Vienna, Peter Révay was extremely offended by his brother's exposing himself to public ridicule.

For Cyprian it had been no more than a casual conversation. Since first wiggling into Rudolf's lunatic household, he considered that it did not matter what was said, so long as people were talking about him. He flitted about in his curly-toed golden slippers through the chambers and halls where weighty matters were debated, peddling anecdotes, organizing secret assignations or diplomatic arrangements. At one moment he might wear the guise of a cleric or scholar; at another he might be Venus at a secret transvestites' ball, swathed in muslin with a golden apple in his hand, and carried high on the guests' shoulders around a fountain that flowed from a fawn's phallus.

"The marriage was a terrible mistake," opined Peter Révay sadly. Thurzó immediately replied that it had been Maria's idea.

"They should never have been advised to move to Holics," continued Peter. Then he suddenly fell silent.

It was hard to know whether this was out of respect for Thurzó, or whether it had occurred to Peter that the disastrous outcome had been inevitable. Or it might be that something had sprung to mind of which he hesitated to speak...

"Perhaps it would have been better if Ferenc Révay had run to the rebels," said Thurzó with perceptible irritation.

Peter Révay just sighed. His brother, he said, suffered from a slight abnormality - or rather he mumbled this because the conversation took place in church.

Holy Communion followed.

This is my body, this is my blood.

Tiny rays of light played bravely on the white, puritanical walls.

"A simple operation would have helped...but he postponed it. I spoke with him about it before his wedding."

"If that's the case...," interjected Thurzó, breaching the unwritten rule about whispering in church. He stared at the other in surprise.

Peter Révay nodded, shrugged his shoulders and looked straight ahead.

They did not speak about it again. Or perhaps just once more, by reference to Susanna's fate.

"To live so shut off, with no purpose...," Thurzó had begun. But whatever Thurzó might think of life's fresh, warm dough, could lack of purpose really be an empty hand? Empty love? Was it imaginable? Or only from his point of view?

"Are we not somehow different?" Peter's question of

course was not born of any real soul-searching, just an invitation to waltz around his self-image.

"Nonsense!" Thurzó did not care for this new line of questioning.

After Illésházy's death György Thurzó became Palatine of Hungary; and history enshrines him, along with Ferenc Forgách, as one of the two greatest dignitaries of Hapsburg Hungary, even if they were on opposite sides.

It was not accidental. Perhaps those two offer a good recipe for survival (for those with a taste for it):

"Our hyenas devour all flesh, with the exception of vultures" (Brehm's *Animal Encyclopaedia,* Volume IV).

In his new and exalted position, György Thurzó had to officiate in another delicate case. It involved Elizabeth Báthory, who was both a Protestant and a relation of Thurzó's, and the possessor of a great fortune. First there were rumours of infidelity...that the widow of Ferenc Nadásdy had eloped with some wandering nobleman. This charge could never be made to stick, however, given the advanced age of the accused, so it was dropped in favor of murder, which was at least plausible, perhaps even true... Without waiting for criminal proceedings she was sentenced, then locked in a windowless cell with a single opening in the door barely wide enough to accomodate the prisoner's trencher.

47

Peter Révay went home less and less.

When he did, Maria would chide him, accuse him of laxity, goad him about taking some specious action for possession against his brother. Peter Révay would sink into terrifying muteness. If his wife began to speak, his head immediately began to ache, as if the wind were lashing and creaking open a forgotten door. He had to close his eyes because his temples throbbed. Maria would begin to cry.

"Calm down," said Peter Révay, feeling his inner indifference, its welling icy waves, with terror and fear. This new and hitherto unknown state of mind towards his wife troubled him greatly.

Earlier in their marriage a single broken sigh from Maria would have made his soul whimper. But now her clawing, hurtful words slipped away without friction, like water off his back. If Maria pulled him down beside her in the bed, which for years had always moved him a little, he just leaned towards her nervously, without tenderness. The thread had snapped.

Later on, Peter Révay rarely left Vienna, although he did not examine the reasons why. He hid in his library, struggling with pen and paper. He was writing a treatise on the history of the Hungarian Crown (under Hapsburg control...).

When he was appointed Keeper of the Imperial Crown, he wrote to his wife with modest pleasure; but Maria replied that now at least he could proceed with the full weight of his new position against "the obscene mistress of Detreko".

Maria had spoken about the "outrage" so many times that it had become stale and hollow. Those who heard her nodded with wan agreement, whether or not they understood or approved.

She even went so far as to blame Klara. Once it slipped out of her mouth (or pen, rather) that she would show Klara, she would show her unless she broke off all connection with Susanna, because she was to blame for everything! But Klara only sent a carefully worded note of sympathy by way of appeasement.

It was Ferenc Révay's incomprehensible silence that set Maria most on edge. She had not expected betrayal from this quarter. But she surprised even herself when she heard herself saying, with an indifferent shrug, that Ferenc Révay deserved his fate. If someone had bothered to demand an explanation for her *volte face,* Maria would have had to reply that she did not mean it in a causal sense but as a punishment...because he who is ungrateful gets what he deserves...he should have contested in court for the (insignificant) remains of his fortune...(perhaps she could bear to speak of him only in this stifling, conversational way).

Maria missed her husband. She now knew that something had changed (although she had not found the reason in her years of rummaging about by hand in her baseless suspicion). Something as momentous had happened as that time at Komjáti, the first time they had been left to themselves, the moment when fate took charge and a single glance decided everything. Pale moon and weeping willow, the serpent and the penitent had come together magically. And now once again the earth trembled and walls swayed between them.

Maria was afraid; she was filled with brooding anxieties. For a time she took pains to hide the truth from her children. She wanted to go after her husband, but Peter sent word that it would be better to wait until the spring. Maria beseeched him entreatingly, aggressively, not to resist her will, because her sweet lord was the stuff of life to her.

When the spring came, Maria went to the spa to soak her skin, which had dried out over the winter. She sent her address and dates to Vienna, as if the Stubnya thermal baths might become a lovers' tryst. But her messenger could not find Peter Révay.

When she had given up expecting her husband home, Maria simply buried her hopes, outwardly without tears.

But inwardly she reeled in a whirlwind of unending rebukes. She finally moved to Csejte to live with her relations the Nádasdys, with only Judith (she who on that clear turn-of-the-century night...), who had married Paul Nádasdy. (There was preserved untouched the tiny cell, scene of Elizabeth Báthory's lingering death.)

The last record of Maria Forgách's joyless life is an enthusiastic, even jubilant letter in which she praises the broad-shouldered physique of her nephew, little Ferko.

Perhaps she wrote to Peter Révay just once more from the baths.

48

Susanna Forgách avoided society in the months (years) following the elopement, although once the initial scandal had died down, she was invited by both good- and evil-natured people, mostly out of curiosity.

Her destiny fulfilled, she really had no use for other people. For a while she wished for a visit from Klara, who had promised she would come. But Klara finally would not leave the museum of her ambiguous contentment. As if it were her mission to keep watch, lest the chairs might be switched about at the dining table they once shared.

It happened that Margit Bakics, after careful, exploratory words, sighed one day, "I hope you can forgive me..." Then she told Susanna who that old lover of hers had been - we already know, do we not? - small drawings instead of signatures...a variety of clues... Susanna did not understand why Margit needed forgiveness or precisely why from her. Although Susanna had never thought of

206

her father in that way, this now explained much. The burning candle ends, the unhappy days when he would shut himself in..., that Trencsén business was Margit business. From that day on she did not pine if Klara stayed away.

Sometimes the two women ventured out alone. Margit tried to persuade her to dress, as was their old custom, in men's garb. But then at Holics the threat of Ferenc in the background had helped them to shudder with feverish excitement, with the freedom of a forbidden act. Now it seemed slightly ridiculous. If they made up stories about who they were and where they came from, let's say to join in a village festival, where was the excitement? Whoever they spoke to was a stranger. No one had seen their faces before.

Thus in disguise or not, they went out more and more.

"Are you happy?" asked Peter Bakics.

Yes, Susanna was happy. She loved the man as any one person can love another. Yet she never remarried, although they out-lived Ferenc Révay by a long time. (He choked to death on something, presumably when drunk.)

Why? This is the last question about their relationship which should concern us. Perhaps the man did not want to? (This seemed the most obvious explanation at the time, and typical of these cases...) Or did Susanna cling so obstinately to appearances, that she would let herself be received as a mere guest or poor relation in Bakics' castle, even when it was entirely unnecessary?

Perhaps she was upholding that gentle and forgivable variant of the truth, to which long ago among sacraments and reliquaries she had falsely sworn... Was the outside world so important to her after all? And thus are the soul's manoeuvres proved so banal?

For the most part, just so banal.

This may have played a part in it. Most certainly it did. But that was not the whole truth.

49

Susanna had started walking again. Spring or summer, autumn or winter, it did not matter, because she was not looking around her, but inside herself.

Not even thirty, yet she had so much behind her. But she still felt like a child, her life strapped to the child's see-saw of powerlessness and petty resistance.

Was there anything growing inside? She had planted one seed of compassion while Ferenc lived, and another when he died. But she could find no explanation either for what she had suffered from him, or for what she had made him suffer.

Her life seemed to be rattling along the same road until the end. She had no regrets, it was just that she did not see the meaning of things, what the crossroads indicated.

Could it be (she perceived this at first only dimly) that some knowledge, some broader understanding might open up within her?

Sometimes she was paralysed by fear of this inward-looking state, and wanted to stay hidden in her snail's refuge.

At least she would not bow her head a second time before the awful din of fate. So she did not marry Peter Bakics.

Once when she was walking in the woods in her strange, obsessed mood, something very odd happened. She was singing to herself, piecing together fragmented, arbitrary snatches of song. Then, as if the leaves were whispering, the bushes spoke; the dense sunrays between the branches scribbled bright patterns on the wood and finally these words rose inside her:

THE CRADLE OF GUILT WAS ROCKED
I STOOD FACE TO FACE
THE CHAIN OF BETRAYAL
AROUND MY NECK

and this followed:

THE WIND CHANGED

As if the trees were making fun of her, their dark trunks took on men's bodies, beautiful, tapering men...

The whole thing was like a dream (she touched an oak tree, a beech...), all welling magic, sensual but not physical.

Then she was enlightened in a burst of flame, as the soul can be only if it is truly open.

She became one with the world, but the determining signs were the opposite of before. Then her reflection had been on the outside and was flooded like a river with its banks disappearing. Now she was drawn back to experience the ebb of the *I*, now the world surged within her and filled her. And now as she removed herself, the world revealed a new face. She saw many things which, before, the agitation of her life had kindly hidden.

The failure of man and all creation was perceptible, audible, tangible, able to be tasted in everything. Her magic coat was torn, its warp and weft of compassion and distant frivolity separated helplessly where they had been intertwined.

Compassion grew, whirling and paralysing her at the same time, without any real goal. And still with a thousand goals.

"Are you angry with me?" the man kept asking more and more often.

Susanna was not angry with him, quite the contrary.

It was only the old frolicsome, eternally celebratory

mood. That's what he missed. "Has something happened?" he would ask fearfully, tenderly, sometimes impatiently.

Nothing, really nothing.

She had grown up, that was all.

About the translator: Emma Roper-Evans took her Bachelor of Arts degree in Art History at Manchester University in 1984. She lived in Budapest from 1984 to 1986, working in the Akadémia Kiado publishing house as an editor and translator. She returned to London in the late 1980s, where she worked for the Hungarian publishing house October Freepress. She is completing a Master's degree in Hungarian History at the London School of Economics and the School of Slavonic Studies of the University of London. She has recently returned to work in Budapest.